A PRIVATE AFFAIR

DARA GIRARD

ISBN: 978-1949764512

A PRIVATE AFFAIR

Published by ILORI Press Books

Cover design by ILORI Press Books

Cover Photo couple © tobkatrina/123rf ; background © Jon Bilous/123rf

ILORI PRESS BOOKS, LLC

P.O. Box 10332

Silver Spring, MD 20914

www.iloripressbooks.com

BOOKS BY DARA GIRARD

Duvall Sisters

The Glass Slipper Project

Taming Mariella

A Reluctant Hero

The Black Stockings Society

Power Play

A Gentleman's Offer

Body Chemistry

Round the Clock

Return of the Black Stockings Society

Playing for Keeps

After Hours

A Private Affair

Just One Look

Private Lessons

The Main Attraction

Ladies of the Pen

Words of Seduction

Pages of Passion

Beneath the Covers

Henson Series

Table for Two

Gaining Interest

Careless Rapture

Dangerous Curves

Familiar Stranger

It Happened One Wedding

Unexpected Pleasure

Midnight Promise

Sweet Temptation

Always and Forever

Truly Yours

Say Yes

Picture Perfect

Clifton Sisters

The Sapphire Pendant

The Amber Stone

The Emerald Ring

Fortune Brothers

A Tempting Proposal

A Seductive Arrangement

An Unforgettable Moment

Novels

Honest Betrayal

CHAPTER ONE

"Are the rumors true?"

Carissa York glanced at the man who'd gotten into the elevator with her. Ed Lehane was a man with more hair on his face than on his head. A classily dressed man, with a full beard, hazel eyes and a slender build. That's what others saw. Carissa saw him through different eyes in her position as the head of Human Resources; a divorced father of three caring for an elderly mother.

"I'm sorry," Carissa said as the elevator doors closed. "What was that?"

"I was just wondering if you had an opinion about the rumors."

"What rumors?" Carissa asked, glancing at a woman who was checking her teeth in the reflection of the elevator doors.

"You mean you haven't heard?" His voice rose in surprise, then he checked himself and fell silent when the elevator stopped and the other two occupants stepped off.

"You must have heard," he said, once the doors closed again and they started to ascend. "Everyone's buzzing about it. Well not everyone just—"

"What are you talking about?" Carissa asked, losing patience. She liked Ed. He worked as the administrative assistant to the senior VP, Nathan Cole, but she had a busy morning ahead of her and didn't have time for idle chatter.

"A week ago I made a reservation for four men from Barra Industries at the Stanton hotel."

"For how long?" Carissa asked with sudden interest. Barra Industries had been sniffing around Simus Labs before, and the Stanton was the only five-star hotel in the area. Simus Labs was located in an industrial park in Northern Virginia.

"That's the thing. He said a month, possibly indefinitely."

"Hmm."

"And if that wasn't suspicious enough, I heard from Alexis that the board of directors are having a special meeting on Saturday. She sent out the letter. So is this proof that Barra Industries is taking over? And if so, what's going to happen to us?"

Carissa didn't know what to say. The CEO's executive assistant Alexis, requesting an emergency board meeting meant something big was going on. "I don't want to jump to conclusions, so let me get the facts then I'll get back to you."

Simus Labs had gone public four years ago. They created smart devices for the home, but recently, their web connected smoke and carbon monoxide detector had attracted attention and was likely the reason Simus Labs had caught Barra Industries' attention.

"I don't mean to bother you, but I'm scared. Moves like this are only good for the people at the top. I've got my obligations. Holly needs braces. Do you know how much they cost?" He didn't give her a chance to respond. "If they bring in their own people and I lose my job, I don't know what I'll do."

"Until things are confirmed it is all just speculation," Carissa said in a reassuring tone. At least she hoped it sounded reassuring because she could feel herself trembling inside. A takeover could be an HR nightmare, but that wasn't Ed's problem. She touched his sleeve, pasted on a smile and changed the subject to something less threatening. "Have any weekend plans?"

"I'm taking the kids to a water park."

"Enjoy it," she said as the elevators opened on their floor. "I'll talk to you later."

Ed went in one direction. She turned and walked to her office acting as if she didn't have any worries and smiled at her assistant, who informed her that she had a visitor. Carissa walked into her office and saw a dark haired woman with a streak of silver, wearing a stylish tailored suit and bold gold earrings. Mia Wexler had not only been Carissa's mentor, she'd been both a manager and was now an executive at Simus Labs. She'd fought for Carissa when others, like Nathan Cole, didn't think she was capable due to her lack of not having a college degree.

"What's going on?" Carissa asked taking a seat

behind her large desk, not pretending to offer a plastic smile or obligated greeting.

Mia laughed. "Can't a person just drop by?"

Carissa shook her head. "No, because I was just about to call you regarding the rumor. A rumor I want killed before it spreads throughout the company."

"You can only kill it if it's not true," Mia said in a quiet voice.

Carissa stiffened. "You mean it is? Barra Industries is buying us out?"

"Obviously you haven't looked through your morning mail yet. So I'll tell you what you'll find inside that sealed confidential memo." She pointed to a pile on Carissa's desk. "It's about a ten o'clock meeting that's scheduled for today for all department heads."

Carissa flipped through her mail, found the envelope and opened it. It verified everything Mia had said. Carissa's worst nightmare had come true. Today, in the executive conference room the Barra Industries monster was going to gobble them up. Barra Industries was a conglomerate made up of different industries one of them focused on the area of home security. It made sense that they'd want to capitalize on a niche market, like Simus Labs, so that their product wouldn't compete with one of their product divisions that was focused in the same area.

"If you think about it," Mia said, as if reading Carissa mind. "It's a savvy business move. They had two options. Compete with us or buy us out."

Carissa shook her head. "This is not good. What's going to happen to Simus Labs? To us?"

Mia shrugged, but Carissa wasn't fooled by her calm demeanor. "It depends."

"On how heartless they are?" she asked.

Mia flashed a small smile. "It's not that simple, but we both know that a takeover can be vicious. Some of us will not make it through the fallout. My guess is that R&D and the factory workers will be okay if they want to keep and use the device we developed. However, it's the office workers who have something to worry about. Expect some heads to roll."

CHAPTER TWO

THE MOMENT SHE SAW HIM, she hated him. He stood at the front of the executive conference room—tall, polished, wearing a dark suit, close cropped hair and skin the color of sundried bricks. All he needed was a large ax casually resting on his shoulder. He kept his expression neutral, despite the tension in the room or perhaps because of it. There was no coaxing smile of reassurance. Carissa wondered if he took a perverse pleasure in their fear. He held all the answers, which left people who were the heads of departments—from production to payroll—feeling like kids in trouble with the principal. But no, this was worse. School kids didn't have to worry about what the principal did impacting their ability to feed their families.

Carissa glanced around the room and noticed that the primary fiscal person, Hannah Broadstreet, was missing. And she was a hard woman to miss. She was a woman with big shoulders, lacquered black hair and a lumbering gait who always looked like she was chewing gum, although she never did. She was one of the key players who had helped keep Simus Labs in the black and was a valuable asset to the company. Her conspicuous absence was not a good sign. Carissa glanced at Mia and could see that her friend had her corporate mask in place, but Carissa wasn't fooled by it. Mia was sixty-three and Carissa knew that alone made her vulnerable. She glanced back at the ax man. His gaze caught hers. She didn't look away, she didn't care if he knew how much she despised him, that even if he managed a smile and tried to charm them, she wouldn't be fooled. He'd lost his chance to earn her trust. Not that he seemed the kind of man to seek it.

Stuart Rich, president and CEO of Simus Labs, walked in front of the stranger, breaking their gaze and took his position at the head of the room. He took his place like the showman he was—eyes bright, smile broad. He meant to appear reassuring, but his efforts created the exact opposite. He greeted them with praise and apology. Telling them of their good work, thanking them for coming, although he knew they had busy schedules and apologizing for how the meeting must have been an inconvenience. Carissa blocked him out until she heard the news she'd been waiting for. "And due to our successful negotiations, Barra Industries will immediately take over the running of Simus Labs."

From the lack of gasps it was clear most people had heard the rumor. After a brief silence, the group peppered him with questions about benefits, promotions and job security.

Like a ringleader in a circus, Rich held up his hands, his smile still in place, almost eerily brighter and broader, and said, "I can't take any questions until the end. This is a perfect opportunity for our stockholders and for us."

Carissa felt as if the words 'for us' were an afterthought and she knew the words 'perfect opportunity' were relative ones and conveniently vague. She knew he probably had nothing to worry about but she hated his slimy words and lack of honesty.

"And now," he continued. "Let me introduce the man who'll be in charge of this transition, one of the senior vice presidents of Barra Industries, Kenric Riverton."

Kenric? What kind of name was that? She thought. But his surname was certainly apt. She expected him to sell a number of them down the river. Carissa watched him shake hands with Rich and smile. His professional, plastic smile made her like him even less and she didn't think that was possible. He addressed the group with the confidence of a man used to domination and attention. "Change is hard for everyone. My job is to make it as painless as possible. Two people assisting me with this transition are Donald Burnie and Glenda White."

Both individuals stood and nodded like dutiful, expensive puppets. Mr. Burnie's silk tailored suit was clearly new and Ms. White's diamond earrings could afford someone the down payment on a house. Carissa briefly wondered who they'd annoyed to land them in some small Virginian town when they obviously belonged on Park Avenue.

"Starting now Donald will take over the position held by Hannah Broadstreet, who accepted a generous severance package and won't be returning." He continued not allowing them a moment to even whisper their surprise or unease. Like a maestro, he gestured to an associate and the lights dimmed and a powerpoint presentation appeared on the main wall.

Carissa leaned back in her chair. She knew what his tactic would be, but vaguely wondered if he would surprise her. Men like him always followed the same formula. First, would come flattery.

"Simus Labs is an extraordinary company and an excellent acquisition for Barra Industries. Because of your loyal customer base, excellent smart device products and impressive advertising campaign you forced us to take notice. But when your smoke and carbon monoxide detector came on the market we knew we had some thinking to do and hard decisions to make."

He had a beautiful speaking voice—a mesmerizing voice that could convince you to grab a knife and slit your own throat for the sake of others. She knew what would come next. After flattery would be strategy.

"We had to ask ourselves, do we continue to compete and risk losing our company's market share or do we find a way to work together?"

She had to admire his semantics. 'Working together' sounded so kind and welcoming. She'd expected him to use battle terms like 'join forces,' perhaps that would come later.

"So we came to the conclusion that it would be best for all those involved to begin negotiations. While Simus Labs is inarguably a successful company, it's also spread too thin and its financial solvency is structured on one main product. Which is fine for now, but what about over the next five years? How about ten? In an environment filled with innovation, it is crucial to think with a forward mindset. Let me present you with our vision of how Barra Industries will propel Simus Labs to greatness."

He spoke as if he expected applause. As if his words could camouflage the reality. Instead of looking at the presentation, Carissa looked around at the audience. She felt their worry, their pain, their shock. She, and they, knew that not all of them would have a chance to sit in this conference room next year. Maybe even next month. She flexed her hand and took a deep breath although she felt like exploding. How dare he talk about numbers and percentages as if that was all that mattered. Were they just commodities? Prisoners with number identification instead of names? Things to be shifted around for the benefit of the whole?

How easy and cowardly it was to focus on the numbers, leaving her to deal with the true cost—the lives. The people. The human element of their business, which men like Riverton chose to ignore. She'd be the one to deal with the tears and the anger while he lined his pockets with the wealth he'd gained and polish his plastic smile. Carissa returned her gaze to the presentation, holding back a yawn. Not because she was bored, but because she was stressed.

She blinked then switched her gaze to Riverton. He stared directly at her. Although he spoke to everyone, his gaze remained on her. She swallowed hard, but didn't shift her gaze, challenging him. She knew she should be demure and glance away, especially since he'd caught her not paying attention. But she couldn't back down. She had little respect for him, she didn't care what he thought. She knew men like him feasted on the flesh of the weak and she would not let him take a bite out of her. A man like him had put a cousin of hers out of work five years ago, another, just like him, had closed down a factory where her Uncle had worked. Her uncle had worked hard to distinguish himself from a family of layabouts and losers, the first to own a home. But the loss of his job had led to the loss of his beloved house and the shame was too much. A bullet to the head ended his suffering, but still rang in her mind like an echo in a canyon. But she knew a man like Riverton wouldn't understand something like that, so on her uncle's behalf, she couldn't or wouldn't look away.

After a few moments, he shifted his gaze and Carissa started to breathe again, not realizing that she had stopped. He had affected her more than she wanted to admit, but she still felt a small victory, although she knew it would be short lived. The reality was Barra Industries and Riverton had already won.

Carissa tried her best not to yawn through the remainder of his talk of a 'friendly takeover' and his plan to meet with each and everyone of them in the coming week, before thanking them for their cooperation. He ended his talk with a smile then turned the floor back over to Rich who answered their questions with such vagueness that no one left the meeting feeling that their job was secure.

Carissa exited the conference room seething. "I hate him."

Mia sent her a sharp look. "You don't know him enough to hate him."

"I know plenty. He laced that speech with just enough arsenic to hurt us without killing us."

"He's everything he's supposed to be—sharp and strategic. He's powerful. The true nature of his character will be revealed when we get to see how he uses that power."

"We already saw it. He's cold, calculated and heartless."

"I'm sure he has a heart, he just doesn't show it. He can't afford to."

Carissa sent her friend a look of pity. "Do you think defending him will help you keep your job?"

Mia stopped and pinned Carissa with a look that made her feel small. "No, but I think you were too busy looking around the room to really listen to what he was saying. A lot of what he said made sense. Simus Labs would be vulnerable in a few years. Barra Industries can help us expand. He shared ideas I'd wanted to see implemented for years, but Rich wouldn't budge."

Carissa sighed, she didn't want to face it, but Mia was right. However, her opinion of Riverton remained steadfast, but she kept that information to herself. She gathered her staff in one of the smaller conference rooms near HR and shared the logistics of the takeover, giving them the letter Rich and Riverton—or rather their assistants— had drafted, telling them about upcoming changes and trying to answer questions she couldn't really answer.

After dismissing her staff, Carissa returned to her office thinking of all the possible scenarios and decisions she'd have to make. She was jotting down a note to visit Ed when someone knocked on her office door.

"Come in," she said forcing a smile to greet whoever entered.

The henchman did.

Her smile fell, but her heartbeat rose. He looked large, cool and polished in a suit that had probably never travelled this far south before.

"May I speak to you for a moment?" he asked with a polite sincerity that surprised her. She'd expected a subtle demand.

She gestured to a seat. "Of course, Mr. Riverton."

He sat. "Call me Kenric."

Seriously? With a straight face? Not happening. "How may I help you?"

"At the meeting I could see that my speech didn't go down well with you."

And you care, because? She clasped her hands together on her desk and nodded as if giving his statement due consideration. "Hmm."

"My job is to allay any worries and concerns and I don't feel I succeeded conveying that to you. You seem very worried." He paused. "More than the rest."

"I apologize. I'll take care to guard my emotions more carefully next time." *If there is one.*

He leaned back. "That's not why I'm here. I don't want you to hide how you feel. I want to know why."

"Why I'm worried?" she asked just to clarify.

He nodded.

"You already know the answer to that."

"I'd prefer to hear it from you."

"What you want to hear from me is how worried I am about the fate of the company, the market and all that you discussed, but that doesn't faze me because," she quickly added, anticipating his question, "unlike you, I don't deal with numbers, I deal with people. The human factor. The fuzzy science of emotion. You have the luxury of cutting this or cutting that without seeing the impact, but telling someone who's worked at Simus Labs for years that they no longer have a job will be painful for me."

She took a deep breath and clasped her hands tighter. "I am excellent at my job, but I can't do the hard part of letting people go with a smile or insincerity. I am worried about the lives that will be changed by this takeover, the health and wellbeing both mentally and physically of the people affected by your so called 'friendly' takeover, because there's nothing friendly about losing a job."

He blinked with all the interest of a man listening to a weather report. She could be fired right now and although she was afraid—she had an apartment she loved and bills due—she knew a part of her would be relieved. She didn't think she could stomach working under such a man.

Riverton crossed his legs and glanced around her office. "I knew I wouldn't be popular," he said with an unmistakable tone of amusement. "I didn't take this job for that and I know acquisitions come with feelings of distrust." His gaze met hers. "But you can't stand me, can you? Not just what I do or what I represent, but me." He rested a hand on his chest, but although the motion was casual it really was a challenge as was his granite hard gaze.

Carissa wanted to agree with him, but she knew she couldn't admit her true feelings and keep her job. Besides, her personal feelings didn't matter, there were others she had to consider. "I'm afraid there's been a misunderstanding."

He narrowed his eyes, but she could tell nothing from his expression. She could only hope he would swallow her lie or at least let it pass. He seemed like the kind of man who could ignore what he didn't want to hear. After a long moment, he nodded. "Yes, my apologies. So I can depend on you," he said more as a statement than a question.

"Yes." She wanted to say no. *No, you cannot depend on me to make this transition smooth. No, you can't depend on me to quiet the herd so that you can swing your ax.* But if she wasn't here there was no one else to look after the employees—people like her uncle. So she kept her composure and said what was expected. "Of course."

He nodded then opened his briefcase and took out a piece of paper. He scanned it for a second then handed it to her. "I need the personnel files on these people. Bring them to my office tomorrow—ten o'clock sharp. I'm on the top floor, third office on your right." He stood. "I look forward to our first meeting." He held out his hand.

Carissa reluctantly shook it, oddly disturbed by how soft his hand felt. For some reason she'd expected calluses. "Yes."

Once he'd gone, Carissa looked at the paper and saw a list of names. Eight names with their positions in the company listed next to them. Her heart fell when she saw the sixth name: Mia Wexler.

CHAPTER THREE

"Does this spinach taste fresh to you?"

"Did you even hear a word I said?" Carissa asked her boyfriend, Morris Howell, hoping not to sound as shrill and angry as she felt. She sighed. She'd just spent the last several minutes sharing how terrible her day had been and her fears of upcoming layoffs and how much she wanted to weep. She'd shared the awful feeling she felt that she might lose her job and how that didn't bother her as much as the thought of telling her mentor that she'd soon be out of work. She's laid her heart bare and all he could think about was his salad. She'd thought a dinner date at a nice restaurant would have lightened her mood, but so far he was proving her wrong.

"Yea, sure," he said frowning down at the spinach leaf on his fork. "I'm just trying to figure out where this puts us."

"Excuse me?"

He glanced up at her. "Why? Did you pass gas or something?"

"No," Carissa said through clenched teeth. "I don't understand what you're talking about."

He returned his gaze to his spinach and shrugged, clearly making the decision that the spinach was edible, then put it in his mouth and chewed. "Maybe it's the dressing."

She knew he could be particular about his food. He was particular about a lot of things like how his clothes were pressed, the thread his tailor used, the temperature in his house, but she wasn't in the mood. "Do you want to be left alone?" she asked.

He set his fork down. "No, sorry." He reached across the table and squeezed her hand with a half smile of apology.

She felt her annoyance fade. "That's okay."

"It's just that if you lose your job, that's going to affect our five year plan." He picked up his fork again and stabbed at his spinach salad. "The lack of income would put more pressure on me, but you're resourceful so I don't see you unemployed for too long. Maybe a month."

"Morris," she said with a low warning.

"Okay three."

"Morris," she said again, feeling her annoyance return.

"You're right," he said wiping the corner of his mouth with a napkin. "You might not lose your job at all and there's nothing to worry about. In another year we can confidently buy a house then get married."

Carissa stared at the attractive man in front of her,

reminding herself that she loved him. Most of the times. But at times like this, she wasn't even sure she liked him very much. She knew he was a good choice. Great marriage material. After two failed ones, she should know. He was gainfully employed and liked to think ahead. Neither of her exes had and she felt privileged that he'd looked past her lack of a college degree. Most men she'd been interested in couldn't see past that supposed flaw. He also saw past her blue collar background. She knew on paper they looked like an odd match. He was a PhD candidate from an upper middle class family. She'd come from a blue collar background, was twice divorced without a degree.

The men she was interested in usually only saw her high school diploma, blue collar background and two divorces. She'd married early, right out of high school because she'd wanted to get out of her father's house. That marriage fell apart when her husband's side business, as a drug dealer, got him put away. Her second marriage was to a man who was twenty years her senior and lasted five years, until she started having her own opinions. Like her father, he didn't like that. He liked his women quiet and subservient, but by twenty-six she was ready to speak. She left him and started as an administrative assistant at Simus Labs working her way up to her current position. At thirty-four, she was one of the youngest department heads in the firm, but she had proven herself. She liked the freedom of having her own money and living her own life. But at times, she felt caught in two worlds. One world where she aspired to be and the other one in which she lived.

She'd liked Morris because he was so unlike her exes. He was always thinking ahead, but sometimes too much so. Like now, she just wanted him to support her, she wanted to share how she felt, not reflect on how what was happening would impact their future. And for the first time she wondered if she really had a future with him.

"What if I quit?" she asked keeping her gaze focused on her plate.

Morris smiled as if she'd said an amusing witticism. "But you won't."

"What if I did?"

"Actions like that are done by reckless or lazy people. Not people like us."

People like us. At least he'd put them in the same category. That was good right? "So you'd be angry."

"I know takeovers are stressful," he said, reaching over and squeezing her hand again, but this time instead of soothing her, she felt more annoyed. "But you have to be calm."

She pushed the food around on her plate. "I hate the man I'll have to work with."

"You're not being paid to like him."

True. His words were practical and reasonable, that's why she liked him. That's why he was successful. Unfortunately, right now she didn't care about being practical, she wasn't in the mood. She lifted her gaze to meet his. "I'd like to get married now."

"I told you that—"

"It's been three years. We can afford to get married."

"Fine, you want to move in together. Let's—"

Carissa shook her head. "I didn't say move in, I said

get married."

Morris adjusted his tie in a quick, smooth movement then leaned back in his chair. "I don't see what the rush is. You've already done it twice."

Again his words rang true, but for the first time they hurt. Because, although they were factual, this time the tone was tinged with an emotion she hadn't heard before —judgment. And as she looked at this successful man she decided to be practical and rational also and face the truth. "You don't want to marry me, do you?"

"I never said that."

"Then why do you keep mentioning my divorces? Do you think I've forgotten that I've had two marriages crash and burn? Do you think it's stupid of me to want to pledge my life to yours?"

"Look, nowadays marriage is just a piece of paper. You know I'm committed to you," he said leaning forward and reaching for her hand.

This time she moved it out of reach. "You don't have to pretend anymore. I'm giving you a way out."

"I don't want a way out. I've invested three years into this relationship. Move in. I'm asking you to live with me, how much more of a commitment do you want?"

Carissa stood to leave, wanting to laugh and cry at the same time. "Obviously a lot more than you can give."

"What are you doing?" he asked watching her put on her coat.

"What does it look like?"

"At least wait for the bill so we can split the cost."

So like him, always missing the big signs for the minu-tiae. It didn't matter that she was breaking up with him or that she was angry. He didn't want to pay for her grilled chicken salad. She pulled out a fifty. "This should cover it."

He pulled out his wallet. "I have some change—"

She grabbed her handbag. "Goodbye Morris."

"I'll call you later."

She swallowed a scream. He still didn't get it. She sat down in front of him and clasped her hands together. "Morris, this is what we call a break up. There is no need for you to text me or call me because we're no longer a couple. I will pack whatever items you have at my place and mail them to you. I'd request you do the same."

"You don't know what you're saying."

"Of course I do."

"It would be cheaper to drop them by."

She shook her head then started to stand. He grabbed her arm, forcing her back down. "You can't do this to me."

"Let go."

"I put up with a lot to make this relationship work. I don't want to start all over again with someone else. I don't know what I did wrong, but you owe me a second chance."

"I don't—"

"Is there somebody else? Is that why you're finding an excuse to break up with me?"

"It's not an excuse."

"Then what is it? I haven't changed. You know what I want. You know I'm not ready to get married, yet you're using emotional blackmail to get what you want. It's not like you to be this selfish."

"That's not—"

He let her arm go. "I said I'll call you. I'll give you a week to get over this mood or whatever it is you're going through, and then we'll discuss moving in together."

"Morris."

He stood. "Nobody leaves me—ever," he said.

That's when she saw a look of rage she'd never seen before—one that truly frightened her. Where had this come from? He left and it took Carissa only a few seconds to realize he'd left her to pay the entire bill *and* he'd taken her fifty with him. A petty revenge. She hoped making her pay the bill would be all she'd have to experience with him. She didn't want any more drama.

As she calculated the tip, Carissa replayed the scene in her mind and found it funny. He was just angry and defensive. Not scary, she'd known him for three years. He could be petty when he didn't get his way. She should have expected this kind of tantrum. And he was right. It was unfair to push him to change. He'd always been honest with her and expressed what he wanted—and what he didn't want. If he'd said he would marry her now, would that have made her feel better? The problem wasn't him. It was her.

She was bored—suddenly restless. Tired of the status quo. Seeing the henchman today made her shine a light on her own life. She wasn't really important. She could lose her job any day, just like her uncle had, and all that she'd struggled to build could fall away. Her boyfriend—now ex—preferred to focus on his salad than her concerns. Marriage wouldn't have changed that. All she knew was that she felt stuck and wanted a change—a good change—but she didn't know how.

Carissa York was going *to be a problem*. He should have just fired her. He still wasn't sure why he hadn't. Kenric sat in a bar, among the sounds of ice cubes clinking at the bottom of a glass, the low murmur of voices and the smell of wood. He didn't know where the smell came from because nothing around him—from the tables to the panels on the wall—seemed genuine as he sipped a drink not wanting to think about anything, but unable to stop his mind. It was his second bar that evening. At the first one, he'd caught the eye of a woman he shouldn't have and then spent twenty minutes finding a way to escape, and he didn't want to go back to his corporate apartment yet, but at least he was out of the hotel.

He felt on edge, as if something was about to happen. He knew she didn't like him. He was used to that and didn't particularly care. What truly bothered him was that she felt important to him somehow. He felt as if by just meeting her, his life had changed. He didn't know how or why, just that something was different and he didn't want that. He'd worked hard for this. Rivertons were always successful. They got the job done. Then why had he even paid attention to her in the conference room? She didn't stand out. She was pretty, but not head turning with her black corkscrew curls fashioned high in a bun and a shapely figure. Her response when he spoke to her in her office had surprised him. It was more passionate and eloquent than he'd expected. It made him curious about her. He didn't like being curious about a woman. That was his brother's territory.

He took another sip of his drink. What did it matter? He wouldn't be here long anyway. Simus Labs was just another stop in his varied career and soon he'd be onto his next assignment. Barra Industries kept him busy. As one of their many VPs, he was used to this process. Over the past several years they'd acquired ten small companies, so he was used to dealing with wariness and fear, even anger. He'd gotten his tires slashed and once had a woman throw a can of soda at him.

But Carissa's reaction bothered him more than those two instances because she didn't look angry or wary. He saw disgust in her eyes. That was not an emotion he was used to inspiring in a woman's gaze. She didn't like him and he knew it was personal, he just couldn't figure out why.

He knew her background. She'd risen up the ranks through hard work. Maybe she was jealous. That wouldn't have been unusual. He'd learned early that people would try to make him feel guilty for his success and money. His parents had taught him and his siblings that money didn't make the world go round, but it definitely greased its wheels. People like him helped make jobs, but there were times, like mergers, when he couldn't keep everyone.

A woman like Carissa York wouldn't understand that. But it didn't matter. She didn't matter.

Kenric finished his drink then swore. Unfortunately, he was eager to see her again.

CHAPTER FOUR

SHE DIDN'T REMEMBER how she made it home. Which route she took, or if she'd gone through any red lights, but before she knew it she was walking up to her apartment. Carissa looked up at the five story structure with pride. It was her sanctuary. It was the first thing in her life that was truly hers. She'd chosen the complex for its crisp manicured trees and shrubbery, well lit parking lot and gated entrance. But most of all, she loved the windows which now reflected the golden polish of a setting summer sun. It wasn't the size of the windows that entranced her, although they were large and beautiful. But what she loved the most was that they didn't have any bars. All her life she'd lived in places where when she looked out a window all she saw was crisscrossed black metal obscuring her view—both looking in and looking out. Now those bars were gone.

"Carissa!"

She stopped a few feet from the entrance to the

building, turned and saw Ashley Torville, a pretty twenty-one year old with light eyes and dark skin, waving at her from her car window. She gestured to a parking spot then motioned for Carissa to wait before driving off in her orange Kia. Carissa sighed. She wasn't in the mood for visitors and hoped the Ashley didn't plan to stay long. Minutes later, Ashley rushed up to her, holding a plastic bag and looking as if she'd returned from a day at one of Virginia's beaches instead of a hard day at work. Carissa could only hope that she'd changed her clothes before coming here, and hadn't taken casual Friday to an extreme by wearing flop flips, tight jeans and a pink billowy blouse. She rarely saw Ashley, although she also worked at Simus Labs because Carissa had recommended her for a position, as a favor to a family friend. She'd been Ashley's babysitter when her family had lived next door to Ashley's family in the old neighborhood. So when she needed a job, Carissa had been eager to help, especially after hearing that Ashley's mother had suffered a stroke and two years later still had limited speech and mobility.

Ashley stopped in front of Carissa and grinned. "I'm so glad I caught you." She shoved the bag at her. "I wanted to return your container to you. Thanks so much for the soup."

"It was nothing. I could have picked the tureen up, you didn't have to come all the way over here."

"Oh, I know that," Ashley said waving her hand in a dismissive gesture, her bracelets clanging together like chimes. "But one good turn deserves another, right?"

"Well, thanks. I'd better—"

Ashley snapped her fingers then squeezed her eyes shut and pounded her forehead. She used to do the same thing as a child when she got an answer wrong on a homework quiz. "I'm such an idiot. I almost forgot." She opened her eyes then unzipped her handbag. "I wish I didn't have to do this," she mumbled, shuffling through the scattered contents inside. "Damn, where is it? Momma's gonna kill me. I hope I didn't leave it at home."

Carissa glanced down and noticed a small tattoo near Ashley's ankle. It was cute, in no way distasteful, but it just solidified how inappropriate her flip flops were if she had worn them to work, not to mention the tight jeans. "Ashley, I've had a really bad day today, could we talk later?" she asked looking towards the front entrance with longing.

Ashley continued to shuffle through her bag. "I heard about the takeover." She looked up at Carissa. "My job is safe, right?"

"I can't make any promises."

She looked into her bag again. "It's just Momma's so happy for me and we don't need any bad news right now. Yes, here it is!" she said with delight and pulled out a small black notebook and pen. "If you could get a man who was rich, fun and sexy would you want him?"

"I just got rid of a man. I'm not looking for a new one."

Ashley looked at her surprised. "You got rid of Morris?" She shook her head. "Somehow Momma knew. So what kind of man would you want instead?"

Carissa folded her arms. "I just told you—"

Ashley waved her pen, which was bright pink with a

fuzzy head. "Just humor me. I don't even know if I'm doing this right. I think I'm supposed to ask you the type of man you want, but I'm not sure you know it."

Carissa moved out of the way to let two residents pass through the entrance. "Can't we do this another time?"

"I mean, there's no harm in me trying to help you out right?" she continued, scribbling some words down as if Carissa hadn't spoken. "You've done so much for my family."

"What are you writing?"

Ashley held the notebook against her chest. "No peeking, it's against the rules."

"What rules?" Carissa shook her head. "No, I don't care because none of what you are saying is making sense. I have to go, I just want—"

"Did you like my description of the kind of man you'd want?" She bit her lip and scratched one of the words out. "I don't think 'fun' would work for you. You need serious, but not too serious." She frowned. "This is harder than I thought."

Carissa snatched the black book from her.

Ashley screamed.

Carissa stumbled back startled by the outburst. "What is wrong with you?" she said in a low voice, aware of a couple leaving the building and a man locking up his car staring at them strangely.

Ashley held out her hands in an anxious gesture, staring at Carissa as if she were holding something fragile that could break. "Give that back and don't open it. *Please.*"

"Okay, calm down," Carissa said handing the notebook back, surprised that Ashley would be so worked up about such a simple object.

Ashley smoothed down the front of the notebook, as if trying to wipe Carissa's prints away. "I know you have to go. Just give me a description of a man you like—not Morris."

"This is—"

Ashley pinned her with a hard stare. "You won't regret it."

Carissa tugged on the strap of her handbag and decided to humor her, although she was annoyed by the question. She didn't need someone pointing out how messy her life had become in one day. Just this morning, she thought she had a steady job and a great boyfriend she'd planned to marry. Now she had an ex-boyfriend and a new boss she couldn't stand who may replace her with someone else. But if telling Ashley something about an ideal man would end this ridiculous conversation she was willing to do it. "Fine," she said with a resigned sigh. "I want a man who's willing to own me."

Ashley's mouth fell open. "What?"

Carissa laughed at the young woman's expression, glad she'd gotten the response she wanted. Since she thought it was a silly question she felt pleased to give a silly answer. "Yes," she said fighting to keep a straight face. "I want a man who makes me tremble when he says my name, a man who's a bit of a throwback to a forgotten era, a man who wants to possess me and never let me go and... wait you're actually writing this down?"

"Yes, I don't want to miss anything."

"Ashley, I was joking. A man like that likely has psychological issues."

Ashley closed the book and put it away. "You don't have to worry."

"True, because—"

"I'd better go." She kissed Carissa on the cheek and gave her a tight hug. "Thanks again for the soup."

"It was just soup," Carissa said surprised by her exuberance.

Ashley looked at Carissa, tears springing to her eyes. "How could you say that?" she asked, but didn't give Carissa a chance to answer. "Few people come by and visit Momma anymore, but you did. You not only cooked her favorite soup, chicken gumbo with an extra helping of smoked ham and dumplings and delivered it yourself, you stayed and talked to her. And by the light in her eyes, I could see how happy you made her. You didn't talk just to me, you looked at her as if she were important too, and spoke to her like you always have, with respect. For that I can't thank you enough," she said then dashed off.

Carissa watched her leave touched by her heartfelt words. At least she'd done something right and the bitterness of the day melted away. She walked up to her second story apartment and stopped when she saw her eleven-year-old neighbor, Malcolm Hewitt, sitting in the stairwell looking glum. She knew he didn't enjoy summer school, but today he looked particularly miserable. He was small for his age, but lanky with a face that could switch from joy to sorrow in seconds.

"What are you doing?" she asked him.

"Nothing."

"Your mother's not home yet?"

He nodded.

Carissa knew his mother worked hard, two jobs, so she kept an eye out for him, usually making sure that he had his homework done.

"Hungry?"

She saw his face light up. "Yes."

"Come on."

She knew he'd spent lots of time on his own but once she'd invited him over he always had a reason to come and visit. Besides, his company would help stop her from thinking about all that had happened that day.

"Finish up your homework while I cook," Carissa said, as she went into her bedroom to change.

"I'm done."

"Then check over your answers because if I see a lot of sloppy mistakes I won't let you back in here."

He quickly set his backpack on the table and took out his notebook. She liked his company. At first she didn't think she would. His mother was a quiet woman who stayed mostly to herself. Most times Carissa wondered how she could afford to live in their apartment complex. Thankfully, looking after Malcolm was no trouble. She'd made her way through high school babysitting and she liked kids—at least most of them. She'd looked after a few terrors and was glad when she switched to office work after one terrible incident with a kid who could make a monster look like a mouse.

She cooked his favorite meal: Pepper pot stew with cornmeal muffins. She had planned on going to dinner with Morris, so she hadn't planned on cooking that evening. Luckily, she had leftover cubed beef steak, and lots of vegetables and spices. She set the table for one, since she'd already eaten. "Okay wash your hands dinner's ready."

Minutes later Malcolm was wolfing down the food as if it were about to run away.

"Slow down."

"You're the best cook in the world Miss Carissa."

"Don't let your mother ever hear that."

He shrugged. "She doesn't cook so I don't think she'd mind. Remember that peach pie you gave us?"

"Yes."

"She only let me have one slice and kept all the rest for herself."

"I'm sure you're exaggerating."

"It's true. I saw her give two slices to Mr. Travis and tell him that she made it."

Carissa hid a laugh. She'd always wondered why of all the things she liked to bake, his mother always asked for more peach pie.

"That's enough talking, just eat."

Later, after cleaning up the kitchen, Carissa helped him go over his homework then it was time for him to go home.

She regretted doing so because after he left, she found herself alone with her thoughts and they wouldn't let her rest. Was she asking too much of Morris? He hadn't said he didn't want to marry her, she did. Was it so wrong to wait? He was a good guy when he wasn't being a jerk. Was it selfish to want him to be just a little more daring and a little less cautious? He had a right to mention her two divorces, he'd decided to date her anyway and plan a future together. Then why did she feel as if she never really would be a part of it? That the future would remain out of reach? That it would never be 'now' but always someday. Perhaps she was really angry because he didn't side with her about Riverton. The scary thing was she knew Morris would probably admire him.

THAT SATURDAY, Carissa spent most of the day cleaning her apartment, washing the windows until they shined, and as she did so, she thought of how best she could defend Mia so that the henchman wouldn't cut her position. After vacuuming the living room rug, Carissa checked her fridge and realized it was nearly empty so she headed to her car.

"Where are you going?" Malcolm said jumping up from his perch on the stairs.

"I'm going shopping."

"Grocery shopping or clothes shopping?"

Carissa grinned knowing the answer he wanted to hear. "You want to come grocery shopping with me, don't you?"

"Yes."

"Why? You could be playing with your friends."

He shrugged. "I think shopping is more fun. So can I?"

"Tell your mom—," she was about to say 'first' but he'd already disappeared into his apartment. Seconds later he had his jacket on and was ready to go.

When they arrived at the store, Carissa had to squeeze her car into a tight parking space—the only one she could find in the crowded lot—next to a large SUV inconveniently parked at an angle. Inside the store, a voice boomed over the loud speaker announcing a sale on barbecue ribs while customers weaved through packed aisles stacking various items into their baskets and hand held carts.

"Do you want to be a chef when you grow up?" Carissa asked Malcolm as he helped her put a bag of apples into the shopping cart.

"Nope."

"A food critic?"

"Nope."

"Then what?"

"I don't know yet. I've got ten things I want to be, but Mom says I can only choose one."

"Well, tell me one of them," she said pushing their cart through the produce section.

"I want to own a fair."

His answer surprised her. She was about to ask him what other occupations was on his list when she suddenly saw a horrible sight.

Riverton! He was only a few feet away looking at pineapples. What was he doing there and why did he look so ordinary? Not menacing, not cold, just like a regular guy. No, Riverton didn't look regular, but he looked less fierce out of the office. He sported a pair of dark jeans and a cream shirt that seemed to compliment his skin making him look annoyingly attractive. She watched as he sniffed a selection he was holding. He looked a little perplexed but she didn't care. Someone else could help him. She felt something tugging on her sleeve and looked down at Malcolm.

"Miss Carissa, are you okay?" he asked looking worried.

"I'm fine. Come on let's go."

"But we haven't finished everything on the list."

"I can finish it later."

He frowned. "Are you sure you're okay?"

"Yes, I'm—" *About to die* she thought when Riverton looked up and their eyes met. She didn't know why she had such a strong reaction to him. She had a right to shop and so did he. There was nothing he could do to her, but all of a sudden she still felt like running away. He nodded in acknowledgment then looked back down at the fruit in his hand.

Carissa took a deep breath. Since he saw her there was no need to hide.

"Do you know that man?" Malcolm asked.

"We work together."

"Then you'd better tell him that pineapple's gonna taste nasty."

"I don't think that's my place."

"Why not? Don't you like him?"

"No, it's not that."

"That's okay Miss Carissa, if you're too shy I can go tell him for you," Malcolm said and before she could grab him he left. She watched in horror as the young boy walked over to Riverton. Why didn't he sense any danger? Didn't he see how much this man wouldn't care? She hoped he wouldn't get his feelings too hurt when

Riverton brushed him off. She watched Malcolm talking to Riverton and point to the pineapple he was holding then pick one up and rub his hands over the skin then smell it. To Carissa's surprise Riverton mimicked the child's motions then nodded. Then Malcolm started talking and Carissa again grew nervous. What was he saying? Would Riverton tell him to get lost? Why did Riverton look as if he was really listening to him? Didn't he realize that it would only encourage Malcolm to keep talking? She had to do something.

She pushed her cart over to them.

"And she makes one of the best baked trout you could ever eat," she overheard Malcolm say.

Carissa felt her face flush. *Oh no, he was talking about her? Why?*

"Okay, Malcolm time to go," she said.

"I was just telling Mr. Riverton about your cooking."

"I'm sure he doesn't want to know about that."

"You'd be surprised," Riverton said.

"He wanted to know how come I know so much about food," Malcolm said.

"Clearly you're a good teacher," Riverton said lifting up his pineapple. "I've been told this one is going to be sweet."

And if it's not will you count points against me? "Hmmm."

Malcolm looked at her a little anxious. "I picked a good one right?"

"I'm sure you did."

He snatched the pineapple from Riverton and handed it to her. "Check to make sure."

"I'm sure it's fine," she said embarrassed. It wasn't like Malcolm to be so eager for her opinion. She tested it keenly aware of Riverton's steady gaze. It looked ripe and smelled delicious. She knew Riverton would have a very juicy treat. "It's perfect," she said handing the pineapple back to Riverton, a shiver of awareness coursing through her when her fingers brushed his. "Enjoy," she said, her voice seeming to drop an octave.

"So what are you going to do with it?" Malcolm asked.

Riverton looked at him a little confused. "I'm going to eat it."

"How?"

"That's none of your business," Carissa said, taken aback by Malcolm's insistence to keep the conversation going.

"How many ways are there to eat a pineapple?" Riverton asked.

Malcolm stretched out his arms wide. "Hundreds of ways! You could cube it and put it on a pizza or slice it and put it on fish or make a smoothie or—"

"I'm sure he gets the idea," Carissa said.

"Miss Carissa makes a pineapple cake that will make you lick your lips until they're numb."

"And now we've taken up enough of his time," Carissa said nudging Malcolm's arm. "Come on. I have to finish my shopping."

"Bye," Malcolm said.

When they were far enough away, Carissa said, "You are sure in a chatty mood today."

"I was just trying to help him," Malcolm said

checking the aisles for the next item on the list. "He seemed nice."

Nice? "He's anything but nice."

"How do you know?"

"I told you, I work with him, remember?"

"Maybe if you make him your peanut butter cookies, he'll be nicer to you."

"I don't need him to be nice to me."

And the last thing she'd ever do was cook for him.

So, she could cook, Kenric thought with a smile as he set his shopping bag in the trunk of his car and closed it. For some reason he liked the thought of her cooking. He could use a nice home cooked meal, but knew that wasn't going to happen. He didn't cook and none of the women he dated did either. Most of his meals came out of a restaurant kitchen or was created at the hands of a personal chef. Not that he could complain. The food was always stellar, but one thing he missed as a boy was the intimacy of a specially prepared meal. At times he envied those who talked about their grandmother's chicken chowder or an aunt's roasted potatoes with chives. He wanted to know what food tasted like when it was made with love. What it was like to eat fresh food prepared just for him in a simple kitchen.

Kenric settled inside his car. The closest he'd come to having the feeling of a home cooked meal was the summer he'd turned eight. At their family vacation home, he'd met the first chef who hadn't gotten angry when

Kenric snuck into the kitchen—a habit he'd started at age four—to watch him work. As long as he stayed a safe distance away, the chef—a big man with a bushy mustache and skin the color of pressed olives—let Kenric watch him chop, slice, fillet, broil and simmer. Kenric watched the chef as if he were a magician as he took ordinary objects and turned them into beautiful dishes. He loved the bright reds, orange, purple, greens and blues of the varied fruits and vegetables he would see lined up on the kitchen table and counter. He loved the savory aroma of onions sizzling in a pan or the light steam rising from a cherry pie cooling on the table. Once, he'd let Kenric crush fresh mint leaves and he still remembered the lingering scent on his fingers. However, once his mother found him hanging around the kitchen she put an end to his escapades.

But by then the kitchen was no longer just a curiosity for him, but a special place. It stirred up something in him he'd never managed to recapture. He knew it was a silly notion to try, but he couldn't stop himself. Over the years, he'd gotten rid of three personal chefs because their austere, almost clinical approach to food annoyed him. He envied Malcolm's joy as he recalled Carissa's cooking, because for a brief moment in his life he'd wanted to know what that sensation was like. And now that eagerness had returned. He wanted to know what Carissa's baked trout and pineapple cake tasted like, and her...

He shook his head determined to halt his dangerous thoughts. He turned on the ignition and put his car in gear. No, he knew better than to let his mind wander into dangerous territory. Carissa York was not on the menu.

"You don't have to help me put things away."

"That's okay Miss Carissa I like to help." Malcolm glanced at the clock. "Man, it's almost lunch time. I wonder what Mom's made. I don't think she went grocery shopping yet."

Carissa grinned, catching the not too subtle hint. "Okay, you finish putting things away and I'll start lunch."

She cooked up a quickie casserole, consisting of cheese and bacon strips with diced potatoes. As she was putting the dish on the table, her cell phone buzzed. She grabbed it and saw a text message from her sister-in-law who lived two floors up. She was almost eight months pregnant. When she saw the message, her heart stopped. It said: Come quick!

CHAPTER FIVE

Carissa raced up the stairs, wishing she'd kept up her fitness workout; Malcolm following close behind. She knocked on the door to her sister-in-law's apartment, then turned the knob. It easily opened in her hands although she'd told her sister- in- law to keep it locked. "Lina?" she said rushing into the living room. She looked around the exquisitely decorated apartment. "Are you okay? Do you need me to call the ambulance?"

She heard the toilet flush and then Lina came into the room. "Sorry I kept you waiting. I swear I have to pee every hour. One sip of water and it's Niagara Falls."

"But what's wrong?" Carissa asked, surprised by her sister-in-law's calm behavior.

She blinked her pretty, naturally long lashes. "Nothing's wrong."

"You told us to come quick," Malcolm said, voicing Carissa's irritation.

"I didn't tell you to come. Why are you always together?" She grinned. "Does someone have a crush?"

"Leave him alone," Carissa said. "Now tell me what's wrong?"

She headed for the kitchen. "I made some coleslaw the other day. I wanted you to have it before it spoiled."

Carissa gritted her teeth. Lina had done this to her before and she was annoyed that she'd fallen for it again. And she kept falling for it. These incidents were only getting worse and more frequent the closer it came to her due date. She'd had Carissa scrambling to her room the first day she was no longer able to see her feet after sending a text that said: OH NO!; the day she'd dropped the TV remote and accidently kicked it under the sofa and couldn't reach it; the day she sent a text that said 'BIG NEWS!' when she'd found out she was having a boy instead of a girl and burst into tears.

She'd warned her to stop, but every time Carissa got a text she still came running. "How many times have I told you not to send me panicky messages like that? I thought you were in serious trouble."

"I'm sorry."

And she knew Lina was sorry, at least for the moment, but they rarely lasted. Carissa's brother, Glenn, liked to spoil her and it was easy to see why. She was as perky and cute as a cheerleader with eyes as adorable as a kitten. She'd secured a major status coup by being the first one, on either side of the family, to bring in a grandchild so she was doted on from both sides. Yet all the attention didn't seem to be enough.

"Did you ever read the story of *The Boy Who Cried Wolf?*" Malcolm said.

Lina took a seat on the lush leather couch. "The boy who cried what?"

"You're playing with fire," Carissa said determined to be more direct. "One time you're going to call me and I may not come because I won't believe you."

"I wasn't lying I didn't...wait, where are you going?"

Carissa put her hand on the doorknob. "I have to reheat Malcolm's lunch."

"Isn't he old enough to make it himself?"

He shot her an ugly look.

"It's just that you're a busy woman," she added. "It's not like you still have to babysit to make money."

"I'm not babysitting," Carissa said.

"I help her out," Malcolm said clearly offended.

Lina flashed an indulgent smile. "Sure you do, honey."

He narrowed his eyes and gripped his hands into fists.

"We're going," Carissa said.

Lina shook her head. "No, don't do that."

"Why not? And you'd better not mention that damn coleslaw."

Lina covered her ears and winced as if in pain. "There's no need to swear." She let her hands fall to her lap. "It's just that you both just got here and I'd hate for you to go so soon." She sighed dramatically. "Glenn is away and I'm so bored. Oh, wait, there is something I wanted to show you." She stood and started to lift up her blouse.

Carissa quickly covered Malcolm's eyes. "What are you doing?"

"I want to show you some artwork silly. I'm not doing a striptease."

Carissa slowly removed her hand from Malcolm's eyes and they both stared at the landscape painting on Lina's belly.

"I wanted to show you before I washed it away. He's a top local artist. Isn't it gorgeous?"

The painting was nice, but Carissa had seen better work at a yard sale. She didn't even want to ask how much Lina had paid for it. "You could have just taken a picture."

"Pictures aren't the same, what do you think museums are for?"

"And you are my living masterpiece," a new voice said.

They all turned and saw Glenn closing the door.

Lina beamed. "Oh baby you're so sweet."

"Not as sweet as you."

He grabbed her and they started to kiss, looking like the perfect couple they were. Her fine good looks matching his strong, handsome features.

Malcolm made gagging noises and Carissa agreed. "Let's go," she said under her breath.

The couple had moved into her building because Glenn wanted Carissa to keep an eye on Lina and the rest of the family agreed, although she couldn't understand why. Lina had two sisters of her own, but when Glenn asked she'd said yes. She now regretted the offer to help.

Malcolm headed to his apartment.

"Where are you going? Don't you want lunch?"

"I can make it myself."

She grabbed the back of his shirt. "Don't listen to anything Lina says. I like your company, okay?"

He looked at her unsure. "You mean it?"

"Yes. If I can get rid of Morris I'd have no problem getting rid of you, if I wanted to. Which I don't."

Malcolm made a low hissing sound then pumped his fist in the air.

Carissa looked at him confused. "What's that for?"

He looked at her and shook his head. "Nothing. Come on I'm hungry," he said before she could ask him why he suddenly looked so pleased.

Carissa enjoyed her lunch with Malcolm and the following day decided to treat herself to a celebratory break-up dinner for one when the doorbell rang. She looked at her spicy baked shrimp dinner, hoping it would keep, then walked over and opened the door.

"Were you really angry with me the other day?" Lina asked.

"Yes."

She patted her stomach then said in a baby voice. "Little York doesn't like when Aunty is mad at Mommy."

Carissa shook her head. "Please don't do that."

"Am I forgiven?" she asked inviting herself inside.

Carissa shut the door behind her. "Only if you promise to stop doing that."

"I promise." Lina turned and looked at herself in the hallway mirror Carissa had hanging by the door. "Oh, I hope I get to keep them."

"Keep what?"

"My breasts. I mean, look how nice they are. The belly can go, but these babies can stay forever." She lifted them. "Aren't they magnificent?"

"Hmm."

"Want to feel them?"

"No."

"Come on, don't be shy."

Carissa held up her hands. "I'm not interested."

"Aren't those Morris's things?" she asked looking at a box stuffed with his clothes and other items.

"Yes."

"Are you finally moving in with him?"

"No, we broke up."

Lina's mouth dropped. "Why?"

"It just wasn't working."

"Oooh your mother isn't going to like hearing that."

"That's why she doesn't need to know yet."

"Are you thinking of freezing your eggs?"

"What?"

"I mean you're already in your thirties, you don't have much time left. I told you we should have gotten pregnant at the same time. Wouldn't that have been fun?"

No it would have been a nightmare. She pointed to the kitchen. "I really need to—"

"Oh you poor thing," Lina said, taking Carissa's hand and patting the back of it. "Two divorces and a long term relationship that's ending, you must feel so alone. But you don't have to envy me. I know my life looks perfect." She paused. "And basically, it is perfect." She couldn't help a tiny grin. "There's no need to lie. But if you need me to help you find a good man, I will."

"I'm fine." First Ashley and now Lina, why were people suddenly so interested in her love life? Weren't their lives full enough? Why did they need to mess with hers? And as glowing as Lina's life looked and in most ways it was—she had a good job, a loving family, a doting husband and soon would be the mother she wanted to be —Carissa knew there were small cracks in their marriage that Lina didn't know she was aware of. It was Carissa who twice had to help her younger brother when Lina's spending had gotten them into trouble.

He owned a profitable franchise fixing and selling tools and small engine parts and also owned a rental property that made him extra money. His life was a far cry from the financial hardships of their past. But while he was making money, Lina spent it just as fast not understanding that although they made more than their parents they still had to be financially savvy. But his sister knew all he wanted to do was please her, which included buying an expensive nursery set and redoing the kitchen. She'd warned Glenn to talk with Lina, but he always brushed the thought aside. One time when she really pushed him he said, "At least my marriage has lasted longer than both of yours combined."

He'd apologized soon after, but she'd stopped advising since and had stopped bailing him out. She didn't know what their financial landscaped look like now and truly didn't want to.

Someone knocked. Carissa inwardly swore knowing who it was. Wherever Lina went he was sure to follow. She opened the door.

Glenn looked past her to Lina. "I thought I'd find you here," he said kissing his wife on the cheek as if he hadn't seen her in days.

"We're just having a girl's chat," she said.

"Hmmm something smells good."

"Yes, doesn't it," Lina said. "Were you about to have dinner?"

Carissa nodded.

"And you always make enough to spare," Lina said squeezing Carissa's arm with delight. "Tell me when it's ready," she said making herself comfortable and sitting down in front of the TV.

"Is Morris coming over?" Glenn asked, following in her into the kitchen

"No, she broke up with him," Lina said.

"Damn really?"

Carissa walked into the kitchen. "Yes, really."

"I appreciate you having us over like this." He shoved his hands in his pockets. "I'm sorry about what I said before."

Carissa paused halfway while grabbing extra dishes. It wasn't like him to apologize for something he'd done months ago. She spun around to him. "You need money, don't you?"

"Just a couple hundred to—"

"No."

"I told you I was sorry. Are you going to hold that against me forever?"

"And I told you I'm not going to help you live in a fantasy world."

"Things have gotten tight and with a baby on the way—"

Carissa shoved the dishes into his chest. "You need to start acting like a grown up. You make more than enough money to live well. You just need to manage it better. I showed you how."

"But Lina—"

"Is going to have to stop thinking about herself and start thinking about your family."

"Are you sure you're not just jealous?"

Carissa snatched the dishes back. "Do you want to eat at my table or not?"

"I do—"

"Then watch yourself little brother because I know you a lot better than you know me. We both came from a father who knew how to tear you down so he could manipulate you. You can try to come close to being like him, but we both know you'll be a pale imitation. Now this is what I can offer you—a way to find an extra couple hundred where you're falling short, but you're the one who's going to have to talk to your wife. That's the deal."

He sighed. "Okay."

Carissa knew he had to be desperate, since he agreed so readily. "Good. We'll talk later." He had to learn to support his family because she didn't know how much longer she'd have a job, and besides, she'd promised herself to stop rescuing him.

Glenn was quiet as he set the table in the dining room. He then returned to the kitchen and said, "I love her so much. I want to give her everything she wants. I want to be a good provider."

"You are, but she has to learn that what you can provide has a limit." She playfully nudged him. "You're a great catch, remember?"

"Except when I'm a complete jerk. I shouldn't have said that to you...about being jealous."

"It's okay."

He shook his head. "I'm the one who's a little jealous. You're so smart and confident. The way I should be."

She waved a knife at him. "Careful, you're starting to sound like Dad again. You're fine the way you are. You're not only the first one in the family to graduate from college, you also got a four year scholarship from the Notrevir Fund, something we'd never even heard of," she said with a sense of pride. That was rare for their family. There had never been a sense of pride in the York line. Her great-grandfather had been just as shiftless and reckless in America as he had been in his home country of Guyana. There was no American Dream story to hand down—no sense of purpose, except to get by, marry and breed. Not necessarily in that order. Her brother had broken that pattern by being the first person in their family to get a college degree. "You are a good man, a great husband and an okay brother."

He rested against the kitchen counter. "Only okay?"

"Yes, when you're in moods like this I have to deduct points."

"I don't want my marriage to fail."

"It's not going to fail."

"I thought dinner was almost ready!" Lina called. "Isn't it done yet?"

"Almost darling," Glenn said, stopping Carissa from offering a rude reply.

Carissa sighed as she carried the baked dish to the table. "She's right. The shrimp's probably rubbery now."

"I'm sure it's fine. Is it really over between you and Morris?"

"Yes."

He sighed. "Mom's going to blow her top."

"She'll survive. In a month she'll forget about me and," she patted her stomach and did an imitation of Lina, "focus on little York."

"You're not giving up are you?" he asked as she returned to the kitchen and pulled warm wheat rolls out of the oven.

"Giving up?"

"On finding the right—"

She held up her hand. "Stop right there. It's bad enough having a kid I used to babysit and my sister-in-law discussing my love life, I will not add you to the mix. Understand?"

"Yes. Although I think I know a guy who—"

She wet her hand under running water and playfully splashed him. "Get out of my kitchen or I'll let you both starve. I'm through with men!" But even as she said the words, she briefly wondered if Riverton was enjoying his pineapple.

CHAPTER SIX

Carissa never thought that watching a man read could be so fascinating. But since she'd handed Riverton the personnel files he'd requested and started reading, she hadn't been able to keep her eyes off him. She remembered providing a brief summary about each person while he looked at their file, mentioning that Mia had worked for the company nearly as long as it had been in operation and that Milo Farmstead had been integral in designing one of their key devices. She wanted to make sure that he understood the power he held in his hands, that he wasn't just flipping through manila folders and sheets of papers, but looking at years of valuable experiences.

Carissa sat off to the side of his large desk, and kept her chair at an angle, not wanting to sit directly in front of him. She looked around his large, expansive office, furnished with expensive furniture and fixtures, but she sensed it lacked something. She wasn't sure what.

Warmth? No, that wasn't it. Color? No, the dramatic wall art added flair and complimented the dark walnut furniture. It was him.

He looked too pristine—suit pressed to perfection, shoes polished to an immaculate shine—odd for such an early morning meeting. But perhaps the henchman preferred the light of day, so that he could see his ax glistening in the sun as he swung it destroying people and lives. She took a deep breath, she'd said her piece and he was looking over the files longer than she'd expected, so maybe that was a good sign. The fact that he was actually reading and not just scanning over them meant he was taking care to consider things. He appeared to be a careful man, perhaps she could use that in her favor. He closed the final file and rested his hand on it and sighed. "This part of my job is never easy, but it has to be done. They'll receive a—"

"Don't say it."

"What?"

"Don't say a 'generous offer.'"

He lifted a dark brow. "What would you prefer me to say?"

"I'd prefer you to say you're not terminating them."

"Terminating?" He shook his head. "You're putting words in my mouth."

"Do words really matter when the outcome is the same?"

"If you want to have fun with words, would you prefer I say corporate downsizing or unavoidable restructuring? Besides, I haven't announced my decision for all of them. However, Mia Wexler—"

"Has the highest respect of all the department heads," Carissa interrupted in a clipped tone. She adjusted her chair and looked directly at him. "She has devoted her life to this company and only has a few years until retirement."

"Now she can retire early."

Carissa gritted her teeth. "She likes to work."

"I thought you said I could depend on you."

"You can, but I didn't realize that meant you didn't want me to express my opinions."

"No," he said slowly, maintaining her gaze. "I never worried about that. But if you can't do this, I'd like you to let me know so that I can get someone else who can do the job."

She deserved that, the sting of his words hitting their mark with painful accuracy, but she couldn't let him have the final say. Not when her mentor's job was on the line. "Mia Wexler is an amazing woman. I know that won't mean much to you, especially when it only takes you a couple of minutes to read all about someone's life here at Simus Labs. It seems callous to me that you can scan over all the work she's done for this company, and just look at her age and qualify her as someone who can easily be replaced."

Riverton smoothed down his tie then tapped a finger on the back of one of the manila envelopes, his steady gaze remaining on her face. "I believe I mentioned to you that my job is hard. I get paid a lot to make the difficult decisions others don't want to. Barra Industries employs more than thirty thousand people." He stopped tapping and flattened his hand on the table. "I've been given instructions to find new jobs for twenty of them." A half smile crossed his face. "See, I have superiors just like you do and I don't always like what I have to do, but it's my job. One of the people I need to find a position for is a forty-two year old woman with three children, one of which has special needs.

"Presently she is working under a man who is one year older and threatened by her brilliance. She has no chance of promotion where she is and most of her ideas are halted. Her only option is to stay put or look for another job. With our acquisition of Simus Labs, I can see where personnel can be reassigned. Mia Wexler will receive a generous offer," he said stressing the words she hadn't wanted him to say, "for her long devoted service. I'm not here to discuss fairness, I'm here to discuss facts."

Carissa fought back her anger and kept her voice even. "And what do you want me to do? Make you coffee?"

"I need you to take notes. I don't want my decisions getting out until I get a chance to speak with those involved, so I apologize for using you as an admin."

She was shocked he'd offer to apologize for anything. Carissa took out her laptop and waited then he started talking about what he'd offer Mia and her anger subsided into a reluctant awe. The man knew his stuff and she could understand why Hannah Broadstreet had left without incident. Mia would be equally impressed by the full medical benefits, one year's salary, plus a settlement for the number of years of service. An amount he'd decide on later. He also discussed her savings and invest- ment plans and other goodies that made Carissa know that while she'd miss her friend, she knew she would be okay. Mia would get a lot of money and although losing a job would hurt her pride, she hoped she wouldn't see it as being tossed aside.

However, after nearly four hours of putting together several detailed severance packages the awe disappeared replaced by the reality of what she was typing. No matter how sweet the pill, the truth was that these people would wake up jobless. With no purpose. Their identity was being taken. She just wanted it to end. Even Riverton's polished appearance had changed. Now his jacket hung on the back of his chair and his sleeves were rolled back, his tie off center.

He looked at one file and frowned then tossed a file on top of a stack dedicated to those to be replaced.

The move looked so seamless. It didn't appear to bother him how easily he could alter lives. The file wasn't that of some man near retirement age, he was a young man just starting out.

Carissa stiffened. "What are you doing?"

Riverton hung his head for a moment as if battle-weary, then looked at her. "You know what I'm doing."

"You need to reconsider."

"Why? Clyde Gelb has missed a lot of time this year. You'd think someone that young would have a better work record."

"Did you even read his file?"

He sent her a dark look "Careful Ms. York."

The look made her shiver inwardly, but didn't intimidate her. She couldn't let it—Clyde was worth the fight. "Because if you had read his file, you would know that he is caring for his mother who has early onset Alzheimer's. Her condition has worsened this year and he's had to take off more time than expected. Not everyone can afford to put their loved ones in a facility or have a private nurse come in and care for them. If he loses this job you could put his career back by years. He'll never be able to compete."

"It's not my job—"

"To care? To give a damn that with one flick of your wrist one person's life elevates while another's life is flipped on its head? Have you considered how he's already suffering and how you'll add to it? He's slowly losing his mother and now he'll lose his job. Do you know what that will do to him? Oh wait, I'm sorry, you don't care. You're not paid to care. Having a heart is not part of your job."

Riverton rose in one fluid motion. "That's enough," he said grabbing his jacket off the back of the chair.

Carissa looked up at him startled, fear turning her insides into knots. She'd gone too far. She'd pushed him too hard. "Mr. Riverton I'm—"

"Come on," he said buttoning his jacket. "We're hungry. Let's grab some lunch. I'll meet you in the lobby in five minutes." He opened the door. "And I mean five," he said, then walked out the door, not looking back.

LUNCH? *Lunch!* He was taking that crazy woman to lunch? He should just fire her, Kenric thought as he left his office. This had been his second opportunity. It was the most sensible thing to do, but with her he didn't feel like acting sensible. No one had ever questioned him or challenged him like she did. He could make more in an hour than she could in a month and she had the gall to question his decisions?

All he needed was her help to make Barra Industries' acquisition of Simus Labs a smooth transition and on paper she seemed like the perfect candidate. A woman who rose up the ranks, was focused on her job and never took vacations. A conformist. Someone who followed the rules. At least, that's what he thought, so why was she giving him a hard time? She knew how these things worked. And he was being as polite and considerate as he possibly could under the circumstances. Why was she determined to focus on things that didn't matter? People had feelings, he got that. However, emotions weren't quantifiable. They shifted. They were gossamer things with no real impact. They didn't last. What lasted were the concrete aspects of life. The things that one can touch and hold. Those were what mattered. What would last after he was gone, after anyone was gone. He sighed and shoved his hands in his pockets, then checked his watch. He wouldn't put it past her to be late just to annoy him.

He felt a light touch on his shoulder and spun around to Carissa's surprised expression. Damn. She was even making him jumpy, he was never jumpy.

"Sorry," Carissa said with a note of caution. "I said your name, but you didn't answer."

He cleared his throat. Control. It was all about control. "Where do you want to go?" he asked, holding the door open for her.

"I don't have a preference. Where are you going? Isn't your car in the parking lot?" she asked as he headed towards the main street.

He paused. "I thought we could walk."

"Walk where?"

He hesitated, he wasn't used to someone looking at him as if he were an idiot. "We can't just walk to a restaurant or something?"

His question seemed to amuse her. "This isn't the city with a selection of different eateries around every corner. We're going to have to take a car. I'll drive."

"We'll take my car," he said then quickly added, "Relax, you can still drive, I don't want to get into any gender issue discussions with you, I just prefer my car." He tossed her the keys, which she easily caught.

"Are you trying to intimidate me?"

He grinned, stopping in front of a car. "Is it working?"

She looked at his silver BMW with trepidation. "Isn't it illegal to have someone else drive your rental?"

"Who's going to know?"

"If something happens—"

He grinned at her over the hood of the car. "Are you planning on crashing it? Keying it perhaps?"

She frowned. "No."

"Then don't worry," he said opening the door. "Besides, it's not a rental, it's mine. Now let's go. I'm hungry."

Fortunately, it wasn't a long drive. Soon they were seated in a cozy restaurant where a guitar player strummed out a lonesome tune, melted cheese on warm bread scented the air and plastic flowers sat in red vases. Kenric set the menu aside and glanced around.

"Aren't you going to look at the menu?" Carissa asked.

"Order for us both."

"What?"

"Don't worry, I'm not particular."

"I wish you'd not say that."

He looked at her surprised. "Why not? It's true."

"First you have me drive your expensive car and now you trust me to order your lunch? I don't even know what you like."

"If I were really picky, I would have let you know. I scanned the menu and there's nothing that disgusts me so just go for it."

She frowned down at the menu.

"The pineapple was delicious by the way."

She looked up startled and he couldn't help thinking that he was starting to like that expression. She looked innocent and cute.

"Oh...uh...good."

The waitress arrived wearing an orange and brown uniform with her blonde hair in two pigtails that made her look older than her fifty-some years. "May I take your order?"

Carissa glanced at him.

He held up his hands as if in surrender. "It's not a test and it's not a trap, I just trust your judgment."

Carissa looked at him for a long moment, trying to consider her next actions. He may trust her but she didn't trust him. However, she knew they didn't have much time so she ordered a cup of split pea soup and half a sandwich then glanced at him to see what he thought, but he was looking at something on the far wall. She turned to see what had caught his interest but didn't see anything. The restaurant wasn't a remarkable place, she was sure he'd been to much grander settings, but they still had a lot to do back in the office, and she wasn't in the mood to drive further away.

She was starting to like him—his steady gaze and quiet manner—and didn't want to. He couldn't be as easy going as he pretended. He should have fired her. Why he'd decided to go to lunch instead was still a mystery, but she was grateful for it. She'd stepped over the line. She hadn't been a professional and that was one thing she prided herself on.

"I apologize Mr. Riverton," she said then burst into laughter at his look of surprise. She covered her mouth, but couldn't seem to stop the giggles.

"You're kidding, right?"

"No, I'm not kidding. I meant it. It's just your face."

"What's wrong with my face?"

She meant his expression, but didn't want to be specific. Especially since his startled expression made her notice his eyes. He had nice eyes. Brown with specks of grey, but she shouldn't be noticing them. "Nothing. Wrong choice of words." Fortunately, the food arrived so he couldn't ask any more questions. But then to her annoyance she found herself watching him eat. He had excellent table manners, revealing the easy polish of the privileged class and ate his food as if he were dining (since people like him didn't just eat) at a top restaurant.

She still didn't like him, but he looked less like a henchman and more appealing, disturbing in a very different way. She didn't like how her heart seemed to pick up pace every time he looked at her. How she liked the shape of his fingers and the cut of his jaw. He was scaring her in a purely primal way. He was an attractive man and that was all she was starting to see.

"Thanks for the apology and I told you to call me Kenric," he said.

Carissa struggled to keep her voice neutral because the thought of calling him Kenric no longer bothered her as much as it had before. "How about I call you Riverton instead of *Mr.* Riverton?"

"How about just Kenric?"

"I was trying for a compromise."

"That won't work because I want an excuse to call you Carissa."

She shifted in her chair and cleared her throat, wondering why he'd want one. "You don't need an excuse."

He nodded pleased. "That's good to know. What is this again?"

"Split pea soup."

"Hmm..." he said staring at the bowl in front of him. "Tastes better than it sounds." He took another spoonful.

Carissa paused perplexed by the look of delight on his face. "You've never had split pea soup before?"

"No."

"Not even for lunch as a kid?" she asked, although she had a hard time even imagining him as one.

"No."

"Well, if you like this then you'd love my—" She bit her lip.

He looked up at her, a glint of humor in his gaze. "You're what?"

"Never mind," she said annoyed with herself for being embarrassed.

"Who is Malcolm to you?"

She stiffened, surprised that he even remembered his name. Then she was irritated by how happy she was that he did. She didn't want to like him. She didn't want to notice how good looking he was, or imagine how he'd look taking a taste of her version of split pea soup. She had to stop her wayward thoughts. "A friend."

"Your little friend had me dreaming about your pineapple cake and baked trout."

Carissa felt her cheeks burn. If she wasn't careful Kenric could end up in her dreams too, but food wouldn't be included. "He tends to exaggerate."

"I doubt it. I'd pay you."

"For what?"

"To make me one of your signature dishes."

"I'd prefer not to."

He fell silent for a moment then said, "Because of Mia Wexler?"

Carissa relaxed. Business was something she could focus on. "I understand your reasoning."

"But you still don't agree," Kenric said studying her.

Carissa cleared her throat, trying to maintain her composure under his steady gaze. "That doesn't matter."

He rubbed his chin. "Let me guess. You think I'm a cold, unfeeling jackass."

She couldn't help a smile. "Sounds like your familiar with the term."

"I've been called worse."

"And it doesn't bother you?"

He shook his head. "Don't skirt the question."

"I don't think you're a jackass. I think you're closer to a different kind of ass, but I'd prefer not to be specific."

"A hardass?"

She smiled. "If you like."

"And why is that?"

She had no intention of telling him. "I have a question."

"Go on."

"With this friendly little takeover that you discussed so eloquently I might add..."

He nodded. "Thank you."

"...I wonder what Barra Industries *really* intends to do with the home device that is so incredibly long lasting. Will it replace its current product that has half the lifespan or will it bury this new technology in the cemetery of other innovative ideas that industry finds threatening to the bottom line?"

"I really couldn't tell you about that."

"Because it's a secret?"

"No, because that's not my department."

"How convenient."

"You're a smart woman. You know what keeps the economy strong. We laud the innovations of companies that allow people to introduce ways to upset long-standing employers such as the taxi and hotel industries. But when you look at the numbers, hotel and taxi companies employ tens of thousands of people. The others don't. There are a number of innovations that would remove hundreds of thousands of jobs and our economy can't sustain that. Both domestic and abroad. It's all about the big picture."

"That's where we disagree. Too many things get buried and lost when only looking at the big picture. When only looking at the logistics of how to get from point A to point B. You're the tanks that decimate villages, the bombs dropped from the sky, while I'm the field doctor bandaging up the bodies of those who survived." She knew her words sounded hateful but couldn't stop herself. She was angrier at herself than at him for her ridiculous attraction. She had to remind herself who he was and what he represented.

He nodded. "You're right Carissa," he said with a note of regret. "This is a war and you have to accept that Simus Labs lost. You must concede defeat and chose another battle to fight. Not this one."

"Can I fight for the conqueror's compassion?"

He sighed. "I'm surprised by your assumption that he has any."

"Just reconsider Clyde."

"All right," he said then smiled.

Carissa felt her tension ease. It was a small concession for him, but a big victory for her. She was determined to get him to see the people, at least some of them, even if it got her fired. She understood his point of view, but buildings, lands and ownership would never replace lives. That was something she'd always stand up for.

The ax man had compassion. That was a pleasant

surprise. But what shocked her more was how much she liked the sight of his smile.

AT HOME, Carissa sorted through her mail trying not to think of how relieved she was that Riverton was reconsidering Clyde or how nice he looked when he smiled. He'd been dreaming about her pineapple cake? He'd never had split pea soup before? She could just imagine the look on his face if he got to try her version where she added...

No, no, no. She could not think about him. He was her boss and they had nothing in common. She was about to throw most of her junk mail away when she saw a lovely invitation tucked in among the pile. She started to open it when the doorbell rang.

CHAPTER SEVEN

SHE OPENED the door and saw Morris holding a box, his face a mask of anger. "Who is he?"

"What?"

He pushed past her and stormed inside. "You lied to me."

"About what?"

"You said you weren't seeing someone else."

Her voice cracked in shock. "I'm not."

"Then who were you eating lunch with today? I saw you."

Carissa nearly laughed at the misunderstanding. How could anyone picture her and Riverton as a couple? "He's my new boss."

"The one you hate?" he challenged.

"Yes." *Sort of.*

"Then why were you laughing with him?"

"I don't have to explain that to you."

His jaw twitched. "No, I guess you don't."

"You didn't have to drop them off," she said reaching for the box.

Morris let it go. It fell to the floor with a sickening crash and she knew whatever valuables were inside had been broken. "I trusted you. I can't believe you did this to me."

"I am not seeing anyone," Carissa said in a quiet voice, staring at the box on the floor, wishing Morris didn't have such a vindictive streak. "I nearly got fired. I had to make him feel good." She folded her arms hating that he made her feel guilty for something that didn't happen. Why should she have to explain herself? Had three years come down to this?

"Looks like he has more money, is that it?" he said in a sour tone.

She sighed. "There is nothing going on between us. And that's all I'm going to say."

"I want to believe you."

"Then try. I've never lied to you before why would I start now?"

He reached for her. "I'm sorry."

Carissa stepped back and squatted down to open the box. "Just go."

He bent down and touched her shoulder, his voice filled with remorse. "I hope it's not—"

She shrugged his hand away. "Goodbye Morris."

He stood for a few seconds longer, but when she didn't move—didn't look at him, didn't open the box just stayed crouched down—he took the hint and left.

Once he was gone Carissa ripped open the box, her heart twisting at the thought of the extent of the damage.

As she feared, a beautiful picture frame with a photo of the two of them on the beach, had been broken. But that hadn't hurt as much as seeing the delicate vase she'd bought herself after her first promotion. It was one of the first luxury items she'd treated herself to. Something she'd given herself as she rebuilt her life after the failure of her second marriage. Morris had known what it meant to her. Although he'd teased her about her 'ugly' little vase, he'd let her put fresh flowers in it when she came over to his place to stay.

For the first time Carissa let herself realize that Morris wasn't just petty or vindictive, he was cruel. She felt hot tears gathering, but blinked them away. She wouldn't let him hurt her more than he already had.

She stood and went back to sorting her mail then picked up the strange envelope and opened it.

She checked the label and saw her full name: Carey Vanessa York. She gasped at the sight. Few people knew she'd changed her real name at eighteen from Carey to Carissa. Who could it be from? Who knew her real name? She never used it anymore. She grabbed a letter opener and swiftly cut open the gold lined envelope. Inside was a handwritten note on expensive parchment paper lined with finely woven lace. *You have been personally selected to join The Black Stockings Society, an elite, members-only club that will change your life and help you find the man of your dreams. Guaranteed.*

She rolled her eyes. An expensive form of junk mail, what a waste. She was about to toss it aside when one word jumped out at her.

Dumped?

She paused, almost feeling as if the word was speaking directly to her. No, she hadn't been dumped, but somehow it felt that way. She was hurt finding out that the man she'd hoped to marry could so easily believe she was a cheater. And he was the one who could break her things, even though he knew how important her 'ugly little vase' had been to her. She kept reading.

Bored? Tired of being single? Ready to live dangerously? Then this is the club for you. Guaranteed results! Submit your application today.

Application? What the heck was this? She flipped the card over, but couldn't find anything else. The Black Stockings Society? What exactly was it? She sat down at her kitchen table and pulled out her tablet. She went online and typed in The Black Stocking Society. After finding a lot of lingerie sites, some escort services and other unsavory sites she couldn't classify, she came up empty. She couldn't find anything about this so-called 'society' on any social media forums. Were they really legitimate? She couldn't even find them listed with the Better Business Bureau. She looked at the nominal fee. It wasn't exorbitant, but she didn't like parting with her money without knowing specifics. How was she chosen? Who recommended her? What were members expected to do? Why didn't they have an email address or at least a phone number where she could call and ask questions? She looked at the envelope, there was no return address. Where were they located?

She hated coming up with more questions than answers. Why was she even taking it seriously? She ripped the invitation in two and tossed it in the garbage then went over to her broken vase. Just like her life right now, it needed to be fixed. She gathered the broken pieces and put them aside in a shoebox and put it on the table. She needed some superglue.

A trip to the local convenience store didn't take long, so after she bought what she needed, Carissa decided to drive around, not ready to return home. At a stop light she looked over and saw a car drive up to an exclusive restaurant, where a valet was waiting, and she saw a striking woman get out wearing black fishnet stockings, her male companion holding his hand out to her. For a moment she could imagine herself like that. Divine, gorgeous, adored.

Dumped? Bored? Tired of being single? Ready to live dangerously? Then this is the club for you. Guaranteed results!

A loud car horn shocked her back into reality. She put her foot on the gas and shook her head. It was just a scam. It wasn't real. How could something like that be real? But she couldn't take her mind off the woman. Then she glanced at her reflection in the rearview mirror. How did she get to look so worn? How could she have wasted three years on a man like Morris? How could she have fooled herself that he had been an improvement over her exes? Did she really think anyone could really love her? Could she ever be a woman like the one she had just seen?

The thought surprised her. She hadn't even thought she'd wanted that. It wasn't the fancy car or the clothes. She wanted to be admired. Desired. Instead of always being used. Her first husband, her second husband, and now her ex-boyfriend had all used her. Didn't she deserve better?

She tossed the idea aside, but it called to her. At home she tried to focus on putting her vase back together, but couldn't. She could feel the opportunity calling her from the trash bin. What if this really was a chance to change her life? It had definitely come at the right time. She pulled the torn invitation out of the trash and taped it back together, a little surprised by how easy it was. It seemed to mend itself, the tears were almost invisible. "I've lost my mind," she mumbled to herself. "But who cares? No one needs to know."

She sat down and read the questionnaire.

Peach or pecan pie? That was an odd question. She liked both. Why choose and what did it have to do with anything? She frowned. This was nonsense. She tapped her pen against the paper then shrugged. Best to get it over with. She wrote down 'peach.'

Eating out or dining in? Dining in.

Are you ready for husband number three? Carissa swallowed. This was too strange. How did they know about her exes and why would they ask her about them? And what kind of question was that? Of course she wanted to marry again. As unsuccessful as her marriages had been she had enjoyed the married state. She liked the idea of sharing her life with someone. And she'd learned a lot. Then why did they ask? Did they doubt her? But how could they doubt her when they didn't really know her? Yes, I'm ready, she scribbled.

Are you sure?

She paused startled by the question. Then wrote down, Yes, I'm sure.

What's he like?

How the hell would I know? You're the one guaranteeing results. You want me to pretend?

Yes, an unexpected voice said in her mind. She paused. She was hearing things now. She truly was losing her mind, but she was too curious to stop now. She wrote: He loves my cooking and makes me laugh and listens to me. She thought of Morris's look and words and then quickly wrote: And is never ashamed of me and will never put me down.

For some reason she felt vaguely exhausted after admitting that. She felt as if she'd been holding her breath. She realized she'd been frightened to dream like this. To hope like this again. She wouldn't over think it or she wouldn't do it.

Carissa quickly looked over the 'sworn' oath. *As a member of The Black Stockings Society, I swear I will not reveal club secrets, I will accept nothing but the best and I will no longer settle for less.* She signed the application, paid the nominal membership fee, then popped it in the mail.

THIS ASSIGNMENT WASN'T SUPPOSED to be hard, Kenric thought ripping off his tie as he entered his bedroom. It had been two days since his lunch with Carissa, but for some reason he felt restless and on edge. Something still wasn't right. Giving a severance package to someone like Mia Wexler was supposed to be routine. Fortunately, being the classy lady she was, Wexler made his job easy or at least tried to with her corporate smile and professional charm. She agreed to train her replacement over the next several weeks. It was done. But somehow he didn't feel it was over. It bothered him. It shouldn't have, but it did.

Carissa York had made him start second guessing himself. He'd even scrambled to come up with a reason to keep Clyde Gelb. His superiors were not going to love that decision, but he knew it'd make Carissa happy.

When had that started to matter to him? Why did he care what Carissa thought? And why did Wexler and the rest of the individuals he had to let go stay in his mind? Why did Wexler start making him wonder about his own future? About growing older? He worked hard to be the best, but he couldn't stop time. One day he'd be in his sixties and he'd have to train his replacement. He didn't like that idea. *That's why you lead, you don't follow*, he could hear his father say. No one in his family could understand why he hadn't joined the family business where there was a guaranteed position for life. But he'd wanted to set out on his own, to see if he could make it. He knew he had advantages in life, but it was working with Carissa that he saw how much. How much he took for granted—the good schools, the connections, the insurance, the investments, his age, his health. He'd hate to be jobless, but it would be more of an annoyance than devastating. He had lots of options. He'd never considered those who had few before.

But that wasn't his fault and he wouldn't feel guilty,

dammit. At least he didn't squander his wealth like some of his friends. One bought a new car ever six months, just because. Another, a married family man with three kids, had an expensive mistress few knew about. He wasn't like them. He wasn't spoiled and didn't think he should be punished for being successful.

But that didn't stop him from thinking about Carissa. Carissa and her laugh, and her passionate defense of the people at Simus Labs. He wished he could get her to cook something for him. If she cooked as well as she defended people he knew the dish would be a savory meal. Unfortunately, that night as he drifted off to sleep, he realized her cooking wasn't the only thing he wanted to taste.

CARISSA KNEW something was wrong the moment she smelled baked biscuits. The scent of warm buttered biscuits floated from her apartment as she returned from work. She walked in and heard humming. Had Lina let herself inside? She set her things down and marched into the kitchen then stopped. She saw a woman, but she certainly wasn't Lina.

CHAPTER EIGHT

CARISSA SCREAMED.

The woman spun around.

Carissa screamed some more.

"Don't do that!" the woman said covering her ears. She was a few inches taller with a figure Carissa envied, short black hair and dark mascara that emphasized her almond shaped eyes.

"Who are you and what are you doing?" Carissa demanded.

"Must you shout!"

"I'm going to call the police."

"Why?" The woman looked at her surprised. "Weren't you expecting me?"

"No. You must have the wrong place."

"You're Carey York right?"

"I'm Carissa," she corrected.

The woman tapped the side of her head with a nail

painted a deep purple with black stripes. "Yes, that's right. I'm supposed to remember that."

"I don't understand. What are you doing in my apartment?"

"You should have gotten the notice."

"What notice?"

"About your membership."

"My membership to what?"

"The Society. And there's no reason to shout anymore the shock should have worn off by now."

Carissa took a deep breath. "I'm calling the police."

The woman shook her head in pity. "Now you're repeating yourself."

Carissa pulled out her phone.

The woman snatched the phone from her. "You don't want to do that. It would completely revoke your privileges."

"What privileges?"

"To the Society." She frowned. "Didn't I already establish that?"

"You must have the wrong place. But how did you get in here anyway?"

"Your landlady is so sweet." The woman turned to the oven and pulled out the biscuits. "Hmmm. We're going to enjoy these."

"Who are you?"

"Oh, I'm sorry." She took off her oven mitt, held out her hand and flashed a big smile. "I'm Sara Kitano, your Associate."

Carissa shook the woman's hand feeling as if she were in a fog. "I don't understand what's going on."

"Your box came. I thought we'd go through it together."

"I'm confused."

"You were accepted into the Black Stockings Society."

"And you're here because..."

Sara pulled out her phone, typed in a few words then held it out to her. "Isn't this you?"

Carissa looked at the picture. "Yes."

She scrolled down. "And isn't this your address?"

"Yes."

She scrolled down some more. "And isn't this your application and receipt?"

Carissa nodded. "Yes, but what are you doing here?"

Sara clicked her tongue in pity. "No wonder you're shocked. You obviously didn't read the fine print. You agreed upon acceptance to have an Associate, like me, help you over the next week."

"Week?" Carissa asked suddenly nervous. "What's so important about next week?"

Sara opened the refrigerator. "Do you want butter, jam or marmalade on your biscuits?"

"Can I change my mind?" Carissa asked, uneasy by how Sara had ignored her question.

"You don't get a second chance at this so I wouldn't suggest it."

"I don't think—"

"This isn't hard and it will be fun. Let me help you, it's what I do." Sara beamed at her. "You could call it a specialty."

"But *who* are you?"

"An Associate. I told you."

Carissa held the side of her head. "I can't believe this is happening."

"I know, isn't it great? Let's look at your package."

"Package?"

Sara frowned. "Wait...that sounded wrong, right?" She playfully slapped Carissa on the shoulder. "Thank God you're not a man or that would have been really awkward. I meant your membership kit. It's on the table over there. I'll join you with the biscuits in a second."

Carissa walked over to the box sitting on her side table. *I must have lost my mind filling out that application. What am I going to do now?* She sat on her couch wondering what to do next.

"Open it," Sara said setting the plate of biscuits down on the coffee table then taking a seat beside her.

Carissa opened the box and found a membership card. "Put this in your purse right away. Better yet." She snatched it and ran over to grab Carissa's handbag. "I'll do it for you."

"I really don't think—"

She flopped back down beside her. "What else is in there?"

Carissa looked inside the box and saw a paper titled 'Instructions', three pairs of stockings and a red garter belt.

Carissa held up the garter belt and stared at it. "I don't think I'm a ready for this."

Sara grabbed the garter belt and swung it around her finger. "You're going to be ready a lot sooner than you think. Not many ladies get the garter belt set."

Carissa picked up a pair of stockings. "I'm not sure I want to know what that means."

"Consider it an honor," Sara said putting the garter belt away. "Not everyone gets a garter or someone like me to help them."

"Why me?"

"Some special cases need more 'hands on' services."

Carissa set the stockings down and gaped at her. "I'm a special case? Why am I a special case?"

Sara just grinned. "You ask a lot of questions. They'll get answered, just not yet. We don't have a lot of time, which is the real reason I'm here. We have to get you ready for the auction."

"Auction?" Carissa said not sure she'd heard right.

"Yes, the bachelorette auction you signed up for. You're a participant."

Panic suddenly gripped her. "I didn't sign up to be part of a bachelorette auction."

Sara smiled. "Yes, you did."

Carissa shook her head. "No, I didn't."

Sara's smile grew. "Yes. You did."

CHAPTER NINE

"Just try it on," Sara said holding up a red, low cut dress. She'd convinced Carissa to go shopping after telling her there was nothing in her closet that would suit and having her repeat the Society oath twice.

"This is ridiculous," Carissa said taking the dress and studying it. "What if nobody bids?"

"Why wouldn't they bid? You should see your profile."

Carissa widened her eyes. "You already posted a profile?"

"Of course. We had to pull a lot of strings to make this happen on such short notice. How else would you have been a participant? I'm sure you're going to make a lot of money."

"I shouldn't have let you talk me into this. I shouldn't have filled out that stupid application to join the society. I shouldn't have—"

"You're not going to regret this. You wanted to shake up your routine, remember? This is your chance. You could meet your match. Now go try this on." Sara pushed her into one of dressing rooms.

"I doubt it," Carissa mumbled disappearing inside.

"Plus, you're raising money for a good cause."

Carissa rolled her eyes and put on the dress. Minutes later she emerged and held out her arms. "Slutty enough for you?"

Sara frowned. "Showing a little skin doesn't make you a slut, but if you don't feel comfortable that defeats the purpose. You've been a little too bottled up. You've got a great figure."

Carissa sniffed. That was a first. "I've got figure enough for two women."

Sara snapped her fingers and pointed at her. "Exactly."

"You're missing the sarcasm."

"You've got some nice curves you can show off." She handed her another dress—black with silver accents. "How about this?"

Carissa took the dress and tried it on. She liked the fabric. "Well?" she asked coming out of the dressing room again.

Sara started to reply when a squeal interrupted her.

"Carissa!" Ashley said rushing up to her. "You look amazing! I'm so glad you finally dropped Morris! He'd never approve of a dress like that," Ashley said making a circle around her. "You've got a date? Who is he?"

Carissa sent Sara a glance not knowing what to say, she certainly wasn't going to tell her she was part of an auction. When Sara just continued to grin, she knew she was on her own. "Blind date. We'll see if it goes anywhere."

"I still have—"

"I'm not ready for that yet. One step at a time."

"You have to get that dress or maybe this one," she said grabbing another dress from a nearby rack.

Sara held out her hand when Ashley handed Carissa her selection. "I'm Sara by the way."

"Ashley."

"We tried that one before, but I thought it didn't show off her legs enough," Sara said.

"True, but in this one her cleavage disappears—"

"Yes, she's got a great set of—"

Carissa held up her hand. "Excuse me." She pointed to herself. "I'm still here."

"We know."

A woman approached Sara and held out a blouse. "Could you find this is an eight for me?"

"Sorry," Sara said with a polite smile. "I don't work here."

The woman looked at her surprised as if she couldn't understand why an Asian American woman would be so chummy with two black women if she weren't trying to make a sale.

"And you should be getting a size twelve," Ashley called after her.

Carissa nudged her. "Be quiet."

"Who does she think she's trying to fool? An eight? In her dreams."

Carissa looked at Ashley's size four figure and

decided to say nothing since she was wearing a dress that was a solid size sixteen.

With Ashley and Sara's help, Carissa finally selected a dark blue, just above the knee silk dress with gold spaghetti straps, that whispered against her skin and made her feel like a million dollars.

Ashley rested her hands on her hips and looked at Carissa with satisfaction. "Perfect." She turned to Sara. "What's next?"

Sara didn't say anything, but they shared a look then said in unison. "Hair and makeup!" before giving each other a high five.

Carissa sighed. "You two are enjoying this entirely too much."

"You'll enjoy it too, if you'd let yourself," Sara said.

Moments later, Carissa sat in her bedroom while Sara made up her face. "You're a natural beauty," Sara said.

"I don't like wearing a lot of makeup," she insisted looking at the array of items Sara had pulled out of her makeup bag.

"I know, and you don't need much, but for this event, a little addition will help bring out your best features." And she was right. Growing up, Carissa had learned, from looking at stylish high-class magazines, how to 'look' the part, and knew how to get a sophisticated look. With Sara's help, she showed her how to make her eyes look more sultry, and how to bring out the color of her lips. When Carissa finally saw her reflection, she looked nothing short of stunning.

~

"I NEED A FAVOR."

Kenric switched his phone to his other ear. He'd just gotten off work and looked forward to a quiet evening. He should have known better than to accept a call from his younger brother, Joshua. "You're about to give me a reason to hang up this phone, aren't you?"

"Just hear me out."

Kenric sat on the couch and turned on the TV. "Go on."

"I promised a friend that I'd go to some charity event, but I overbooked."

"What's her name?"

"I didn't say it was a woman."

Kenric grinned. "I know you, it's always a woman."

"Fine. You're right. Her name's..." He paused then swore.

"You forgot her name?"

"She has one of those foreign names with lots of consonants."

"Well, you'd better remember it fast if you want to see her again."

His brother laughed. "I don't worry. I call them 'honey' or 'baby' until I remember or get a hint."

"You're going to get caught one day."

"So will you help me?"

Kenric picked up the remote and flipped through the channels. "What do I have to do?"

"Just show up and bid on 563."

"Fine. What's your limit?"

"Couple thousand. I'll send you the logistics. Thanks."

Kenric hung up the phone then had a strange feeling his brother wasn't telling him something. He found out later what that was when he got the address and full information about the event—it was a bachelorette auction! He should have known his brother would ditch one woman to woo another. He called him right back. "No."

"Kenric, it's just for a couple hours."

"I'm not doing it."

"You promised."

"I didn't promise anything."

"I promised her. I convinced her to try it. I just need you to get the ball rolling. Make a bid so she doesn't feel bad. You don't have to go out with her."

"What does she look like?"

"I don't know. It's the organizer I'm trying to impress."

Kenric turned off the TV and pinched the bridge of his nose. "You're going to give me a headache."

"Aren't you bored? It's only for one night and you get to see pretty ladies."

Although his brother lived in the suburbs, just outside Washington, D.C., like him, he was willing to travel to different states like Virginia to woo his various women. That's where he differed.

"I don't care how pretty they are."

"It's for a charity."

"So what?"

"It's to raise funds for a local facility that helps addicts get their lives back on track."

Kenric swore, his brother had hit on one of his biggest weaknesses. He had a soft spot for people overcoming addictions and admired those who tried to help them. "You bastard."

Joshua laughed, knowing he'd won. "Have fun."

He wasn't going to have fun, Kenric thought that Friday evening as he took his chair at the charity event. Large chandeliers hung above, while the scent of roses floated through the mauve and gold-carpeted ballroom. He flipped through the catalog then stopped at a name he recognized: *Carissa York.* He blinked. No, it couldn't be *his* Carissa York. She wouldn't sign up for something like this, would she? There was no picture just a description, but it was enough to identify her. She offered four home-made meals over the weekend: Two lunches and two dinners. One meal was a hot and spicy buffalo chicken salad with a cheese stuffed mushroom appetizer. He licked his lips, feeling his mouth water. He slammed the catalog closed. No, he couldn't bid on Carissa. His brother wanted him to bid on 563. He took a deep breath then carefully re-opened the catalog and read 563's profile. It was nice, but his mind kept going back to the promise of a weekend of four hot, home cooked meals. He read the rules.

Damn he could only bid on one. He set the catalog aside and leaned back in his chair. The decision had been made. He wasn't here for himself, besides it would make things awkward between them. He wasn't going to bid on 462. He'd just enjoy the show then leave as he'd planned to. He listened to the announcer and watched with interest until he heard, "And now we have Bachelorette Package 462. Carissa York who..."

But the words fell away and he could only hear the pounding of his heart. The woman who stepped on the stage was not the woman he knew. The woman who'd challenged him at the office, who'd laughed at him in the restaurant. This beautiful vision, with her hair styled on top of her head with a gold ribbon threaded through the twists, looked amazing.

Kenric couldn't take his eyes off her watching her every move, as she walked across the stage wearing stylish three-inch gold heels and a pair of shimmering black stockings. She looked like nothing he'd ever seen before. A deep shout broke him out of his trance as someone made a bid.

He could only bid on one woman.

Another man bid.

Kenric drummed his fingers. 563 hadn't come out yet. He was supposed to wait for her.

A third bid.

He rubbed his lip. If he kept stalling, he'd lose his chance. If he wanted an opportunity for her to see a different side of him this was it. This wasn't personal, this was business. This could improve their working relationship.

A fourth bid.

Kenric leaned forward in his chair, gripping his hands together. No, this wasn't about work. He couldn't fool himself. He wanted her.

"And 462 going once..."

He may regret it.

"Going twice..."

But he didn't care. He lifted up his card and made an offer.

CHAPTER TEN

PEOPLE GASPED at the large number, but Carissa nearly cried out. It wasn't the amount that stunned her, but the man. What was *he* doing there? No one was supposed to know about this. The event was being held in another county. Why was he bidding on her? Didn't he realize she felt humiliated enough already? Even though she was glad that several men had actually made an offer, compared to the bids for the other five women who had gone ahead of her, their bids were considerably lower. It seemed that four meals with a full figured woman wasn't all the rage no matter how 'smoking hot'—as Ashley liked to say—she looked. The auctioneer was ready to accept the final bid when Kenric's voice rang clear through the room offering more than any man had for the first five women combined.

The announcer repeated the number in awe then said, "Okay that will be 462 going once..."

Another voice cut through with a higher offer.

Carissa looked towards the back of the room and saw Morris! What was he doing there? Did someone tell him about the event? Was this some sort of cruel joke? Was she dreaming? She didn't know what would be worse to be bought by her ex or her boss. She pinched herself then winced. She wasn't dreaming. This nightmare was really happening.

"Well gentleman, this is getting exciting," the announcer said. She looked at Riverton. "Do you have a counter offer?"

Carissa held her breath expecting him to lean back and shake his head, but instead he increased his amount.

Rumblings whispered through the room.

She looked at him, that implacable mask in place. She wanted to mouth 'what are you doing?' but instead kept her smile in place. She hoped another man would come in and outbid them both.

Morris countered.

Riverton didn't even look at him, coolly offering yet a higher amount.

Carissa could feel herself sweating, if Riverton really wanted to win he could, he could outbid Morris. But why would he want to? She offered up a silent prayer. Morris had to win. She couldn't imagine having to cook for her new boss. At least she knew Morris and two days with him would be awful but tolerable. Riverton, on the other hand, was a complete unknown.

"That is 462 going once...."

Come on Morris say something.

"Going twice..."

You bastard, don't you have any balls?

"Sold to the gentleman over there!"

No, no she couldn't be bought by Riverton. She couldn't be his prize. It had to be a mistake. Carissa stumbled off the stage. Other women swarmed around her.

"You've made the most money for the entire evening!" one said.

"Did you hire them?" another asked.

A third chimed in, "Wow, this event really pulled in a large check this time."

But Carissa blocked out their words, remembering only the burst of applause that had followed Riverton's success. She was not going to let him get away with this.

"What are you doing?" she demanded when she found Riverton handing a check to the organizer after the event had ended.

"I'm not sure yet," he said sounding in a daze.

Morris marched up to them. "I was willing to give you a second chance. I actually believed you and this is how you repay my trust?"

"What are you even doing here?" Carissa asked.

"My firm is hosting this event. When I saw your name listed, I thought you did it for me." He reached for her hand.

Riverton casually slapped it away. "Look, but don't touch."

"What?"

Riverton sent him a pointed look. "She's mine for the

next two days and I like what belongs to me handled with care."

"Yours?" Morris said, his eyebrows shooting up. "She used to be my girlfriend and—"

"'Used to' being the operative word. If you don't know the meaning, look it up." He turned.

Morris shoved his hands in his pockets. "I can't believe you tried to convince me that he's your boss."

"But he is—"

Riverton spun her to him, pressed his mouth to hers—making her senses reel—then sent Morris a look that was both a challenge and a threat. "The new man in her life." He looped Carissa's arm through his and led her out of the room. "I'll walk you to your car."

She nearly had to run to maintain his pace, her lips still hot from the touch of his. Once they were in the hall, he released her. "Sorry about that," he said, his voice deeper than she remembered, his tone making her skin tingle.

She stared at him baffled by both his action and her response to him. "Which part?"

"The kiss. I had to do it, I couldn't have you telling him I was your boss. The fewer people know about this the better."

"Agreed, but—"

"Good."

Carissa grabbed his sleeve before he could turn. "Why did you do this? What were you thinking?"

His gaze fell to her hand then rose to meet her eyes. "I still don't know," he said in a voice that sounded both awestruck and confused. He turned and left.

Carissa watched him leave. Why was he pretending that he didn't know what he was doing? Then why did he look so convincing? He seriously looked like a man who was surprised by his own action, a little dazed, stunned. But that couldn't be. Riverton was a precise man. A man who was always ten steps ahead of everyone, at least that was how he appeared in the office. This man was a stranger. And now she had to cook for him.

She turned around to go get her things. She saw Sara staring at her wide-eyed. She held out Carissa's jacket and handbag. "You were sensational!" She clapped her hands together. "You must be thrilled!"

Carissa shook her head, wishing Sara would stop talking in exclamation points. "No I—"

"And that kiss." She fanned herself with her hand, as if trying to overcome a sudden heat wave. "My report for this case is going to be stellar."

"Report?"

"Pretend I didn't say that," she said then mimed zipping her mouth closed.

"You may be happy about this, but I am devastated."

Sara mimed unzipping her mouth. "Why?"

"You don't know what Riverton is like."

"All I know is that he made you one of the highest ticket items at the auction. And kissed you like you were one of the sexiest women in the room. You should have seen the sudden interest on the other men's faces. They all wondered what they were missing."

Carissa lifted her chin, flattered by her words. "Other men were interested?"

"Oh, yes."

Carissa had to admit that hearing that bit of news felt good, but she was still wary. What was he up to?

"But we don't have time to think about that," Sara said heading to the exit. "You've got to get back and prepare to go shopping for the four meals you plan to prepare next weekend. Maybe five."

"Five?"

She winked at her. "Breakfast may be included."

"I can tell you this with certainty. I will not be making him breakfast."

HIS BROTHER WAS STILL LAUGHING. He'd been laughing for the last three minutes. Every time he stopped and paused, Kenric would say something and then his brother would start laughing again.

"It's not that funny," Kenric said, pouring milk on his cereal. The morning sun was bright but he still had the blinds closed. Last night felt like a dream and that brief kiss like heaven, he didn't want to wake up yet.

"I know I asked for your help, but I didn't expect you to go this far."

"I just wanted you to know I didn't bid on 563," he said. That was the only reason he'd called him. He'd hoped to just leave a message. He hadn't expected his brother to answer the phone, especially this early.

"Who cares? Jackie's so happy with how much money they raised she plans to personally thank me next week."

"What about what's-her-name?"

"Don't worry, I haven't forgotten about her."

"Did you finally remember her name?"

"Oh yea...it's uh..." He swore. "It will come back to me. You just shocked me that's all."

Kenric grabbed a spoon and carried his bowl to the table. "I shocked myself."

"I know what happened."

Kenric paused with the spoon halfway to his mouth. He set it back down. "You do?"

"Jackie told me that 462 was only getting low bids. You felt sorry for her, didn't you?"

Kenric picked up his spoon again. "No. I wanted her."

"Are you serious?"

"Would I spend that kind of money if I wasn't serious?"

"I would," Joshua said. "I like to have fun, especially with plain girls. They're always so easy to please."

"Oh...we're talking about you right now? I didn't think we were."

"Okay, point taken. We're not alike. What's that crunching noise?"

"I'm eating breakfast."

"It sounds like cereal."

"Because it is cereal," Kenric grumbled taking another spoonful.

"You hate cereal."

"I don't have time to get a big breakfast. Besides, I want to be prepared for when she shows up." He didn't want to tell his brother that in a few minutes he was going to have someone come in to clean his apartment and make sure the kitchen was spotless.

"She's not coming until next weekend."

"I'm considering this a trial run."

"I can't believe she's got you eating cereal. Are you hoping to get lucky?"

"Nothing's going to happen. I'm her—" He stopped before he said 'her boss'. His brother didn't need to know that. "I just want to taste her cooking and if you start laughing again I'll strangle you."

"Then I'd better hang up," he said then did.

Kenric disconnected then swore. His brother was right, this wasn't like him. But he was serious, it was just lunch and dinner for two days nothing more. Nothing to worry about.

She hadn't seen him all week. Carissa still didn't know how he'd managed it, but she was grateful, because she didn't know how she'd respond when she saw him again. It was embarrassing enough that Ed hadn't recognized her at first when she'd gone to talk to him and that her assistant made a playful whistle when Carissa had walked in that Monday morning after spending a weekend with Sara—getting a full body massage and facial. What had altered her appearance the most was the seventy-year-old Nigerian tailor, Sara had invited to drop by her apartment and go through Carissa's closet. Although she was an older woman, she carried herself like a dancer. When she opened Carissa's closet, she stared at Carissa's wardrobe as if she'd stumbled upon a tragedy.

"You Americans. Why do you do this to yourselves? You carelessly buy things off the rack and never make sure they fit you." She pulled down one of Carissa's suits. "This is a great style, wonderful fabric and nice cut and it would be perfect if you wanted to end up looking like a box." She picked up a skirt. "And this? My dear, are you afraid of your hips? It gives you no dimension."

Carissa laughed. "Some would say I have too much dimension."

"That is your mistake. You never worry about what others think. You only worry about what you think. Now let me show you how clothes should really look." She took five key pieces from Carissa's wardrobe and two days later transformed them into exclusive pieces, giving her a designer style and flavor she'd never thought herself capable of carrying off. Just as she had done with her makeup, Carissa had taught herself everything she knew about buying quality clothes and styles, for less of course, and prided herself on having a classy wardrobe. But she had never before taken the time to have her clothes adjusted to fit her shape. She now saw how important having a personal tailor was.

"Don't worry," Sara told her after seeing her new clothes on her. "The Society has made arrangements to have your entire wardrobe altered, at no cost to you."

That Monday, she'd strutted into the office feeling more powerful and professional than she ever had before. And it had been great to have others notice, but by the weekend, she felt her confidence fading.

Today was the day of reckoning—Saturday. She'd hoped for rain, but rays of the early morning sun slipped through her windows, bathing her room in light.

Carissa stood in her kitchen and looked over her menu for the fifth time that morning. She couldn't believe what the Society had selected for her to cook and again wondered why Riverton had offered to pay so much for it. She'd spent last night shopping and gathering all the ingredients and going over the recipes to make sure she remembered everything, although she knew most of them by heart.

"I don't know what's got you so worked up Miss Carissa," Malcolm said closing a lid on several cups of chopped carrots. "You never fail."

He had helped her chop, slice and crush all morning. She hadn't told him about the bachelorette auction, just that she wanted to do something special for a friend. She'd needed his help, since Sara was determined that Carissa had to focus on her clothes, make-up and hair.

"He didn't just buy a few good meals," she reminded her as she did Carissa's make up. "He bought a personal service."

She'd helped Carissa select a yellow dress, that pulled in at the waist, with a full, swing skirt, trimmed with white eyelets and finished off the look with a pair of 24 carat gold hoop earrings. Once Sara left, Carissa spent what little time she had left, making sure she had all of the items she needed to cook for a man she'd hoped only to see during the week. And even then, on a limited basis.

She glanced over at Malcolm as he checked to make sure all the lids were closed tight. He was a good little friend. Too bad her relationships with kids were always better than with men. She wondered what kind of man he would grow up to be. She hoped a good one. Not that his mother noticed, but so far she'd done a great job. He'd even given her ideas for her menu, suggesting some alterations she hadn't thought of. She knew what she'd make for lunch and for dinner tonight, the hot and spicy buffalo chicken salad with a cheese stuffed mushroom appetizer for lunch and a rolled rib roast, with a steamed medley of yams and red potatoes and asparagus for dinner. On Sunday she'd prepare a white bean chili, with homemade cornbread for lunch, and poached salmon with a mustard dill sauce and Spanish rice and barley for dinner. As for dessert, she threw in several items, hoping she would be able to come up with something quick and simple.

As she drove over to his place, she decided she'd start the dinner that evening, with a fennel salad and champagne vinaigrette. Since she knew she couldn't back out she wanted Riverton to get his money's worth. She would not focus on the kiss. Although she hadn't been able to forget it, she would just focus on the food and getting out of his place as fast as possible.

CHAPTER ELEVEN

He'd invited trouble into his kitchen. He'd been able to survive yesterday, being as distant and professional as he could as she prepared two delectable meals. All Saturday, he'd kept the conversation light and casual—although that had become a struggle later in the day after he'd tasted a peach tart so succulent he couldn't look at her for fear he'd pounce on her. But it was a new day—his last day— and he could feel his resistance waning.

Kenric watched Carissa set up to prepare dinner with more interest than he should. Today she was wearing a soft flowing light blue short-sleeve blouse over a pair of dark tan trousers. His brother was right, he didn't just want to taste her cooking. First he'd start by taking off her apron. The kitchen was hot, he saw the sheen of sweat on her skin and watched one small liquid river slide down her neck and disappear into the sweet, dark crevice between her breasts. He nearly lost all control when she dropped a dishtowel and bent over to pick it up giving him a beautiful view of her behind. She was excellently proportioned, but not his usual type. He usually liked them fit and trim since he'd been a runner in college, but now he didn't care about that. He didn't need her to run. She was perfect right where she was.

"Sorry, this is taking a little longer than I thought," Carissa said.

"That's okay." *Take all the time you want*, he wanted to say. He silently swore, now he was starting to sound like a pervert. He was her boss for goodness sakes he couldn't have thoughts like that about her. He needed to get a grip, stop thinking about the sweet smells filling the air and the woman in his kitchen causing more than the hair on his arms to rise up. He stood. He needed to get some air. Go for a quick walk around the block.

He headed for the door. "I'll be back in a minute."

Carissa jumped in front of him so fast that he crashed into her. And he felt the soft give of her breasts against his chest. He grabbed her as she stumbled back then released her just as quickly.

"Where are you going?" she asked almost in a panic.

"Just out for a walk."

"Dinner will be ready in a minute."

"I know, but—"

"Please just sit," she said pointing to the table. "I know it's taking longer than you wanted, but it's almost done."

Kenric reluctantly returned to the table not wanting to upset her.

"I don't want you to report me."

"Why would I report you?"

"I know you want to get your money's worth," she said heading back into the kitchen.

"I've already gotten it and more," he mumbled.

"What?" She peeked her head out of the kitchen. "You want something more?"

Oh yes. "No, nothing."

She returned to the stove. Kenric briefly covered his face and groaned. This had been a mistake. He'd never be able to look at her again in the office without remembering the sight of her licking hot, spicy sauce from her lips, delicately adding fresh basil to a dish as if it were a work of art.

"Here you go."

He lifted his head and watched her place the poached salmon and rice in front of him. "Looks delicious." He took a bite. "And tastes even better."

"Good." She reached back for her apron string. "Well, this is embarrassing. I seem to have made a knot."

Kenric jumped up with a little too much eagerness. "Let me help." He slowly untied the knot, for a moment allowing himself to imagine, unzipping her blouse, unlatching her bra, pulling down her...

He took a deep breath and returned to his seat, while she sat across from him.

"Are you okay?" Carissa looked at him concerned.

"What?"

"You just groaned."

"I did?"

"Yes."

He cleared his throat. "Old knee injury," he said

patting it. "But this meal will cure it. Ever thought of catering?"

Carissa paused. "What?"

"You could make a lot of money. I hired a caterer once who wasn't half as good as you and he's very successful."

"I like what I'm doing."

"Really?"

"Don't you?"

He shrugged. "It's just work, I don't really think about enjoying it."

"Why not?"

He shrugged again. "I guess because there's really no point." He set his fork down and sat back. "I'd like to do this again."

"Can't you afford a chef?"

He furrowed his brows. "A chef?"

"Also there are several fine restaurants around if you've gotten tired of the food places near your apartment."

Somehow he'd lost control of the conversation. "I'm sorry?"

"You want me to continue to cook for you, right? That's the one thing James said he misses most in jail. A home cooked meal."

Kenric stiffened. That wasn't what he was referring to, but he didn't try to clarify. "Who's James?"

"My ex. At least one of them," she said with a slight chuckle.

"Your ex is in jail?"

"One of my exes. I married twice."

"What's he in jail for?"

"Dealing drugs. I didn't know it at the time. I never touched the stuff and—"

Kenric returned his attention to his plate. "That's okay you don't have to defend yourself to me."

"From that look on your face, you hate dealers don't you?"

His head shot up, surprised by her words and knowing tone. A piece of salmon dropped from his fork onto the plate, spraying his shirt with sauce. He looked down and swore. First she made him jumpy, now he was a klutz. He pushed himself from the table. "I'll go change."

"It's just a little stain, I can—"

He stood. He didn't want her anywhere near him. "I'll be right back," he said then disappeared into his bedroom.

AT LEAST SHE discovered one thing, Riverton didn't like drug dealers. She hadn't been able to figure out much about him over the past two days. He kept the conversation flowing, but revealed little about himself, except today. The look of revulsion on his face spoke volumes. She might as well have said she'd been married to a murderer. Maybe that was why he was at the charity event. He probably wanted to support their victims. She wondered why it was such a tender spot for him. Over the past two days she'd started to wonder a lot. She no longer saw him as a henchman. He was easy to talk to and loved her cooking.

No, 'loved' seemed to be too tame a word. Adored sounded better. No one—not even her two exes—had ever approached her food with such reverence. Riverton didn't lick his fingers or his lips, he was too refined for that, but he approached her food like a saint at the footsteps of a grand cathedral. For a brief moment she'd wanted to be his spoon as he seemed to caress the bowl of white bean chili she'd made for lunch until it was completely gone.

Although she was certain he was used to fancier fair, he ate her meals as if he were dining at a five star restaurant. He complimented her, using some adjectives she'd never even heard before. But even though she didn't know their exact meaning the look on his face said it all, and the flush of pleasure that followed his words and the light in his brown gaze, let her know she was treading on dangerous ground. However, that didn't stop her from being disappointed that tonight would be their last meal together. She wondered what other dishes he might like and thought of her signature Red BBQ coleslaw and potato salad.

She heard the doorbell.

"Someone's at the door!" she called out to him. "Do you want me to answer it?" When she didn't hear a reply, Carissa went to the door and opened it.

A tall, striking looking man stood there. He tossed her his coat. "Is Kenric around?"

"He's getting changed," she said as the man waltzed past her.

He flopped down on a chair. "Hmm, something smells divine and I'm starving. Did you make extra?"

"Well…"

"Something cool to start things off would be nice as well," he said kicking off his shoes and resting his feet on the coffee table.

She didn't know who he was, but he certainly was messy. Carissa moved his shoes out of the way and hung up his coat then poured him some lemonade. She didn't know whether to feed him though. She went to Riverton's room and knocked, wondering what was taking him so long.

"I'll be right out," he said.

"There's someone here to see you."

The door swung open. He looked at her surprised. "To see me?"

She was just as surprised at the sight of him with his shirt open, revealing a muscular chest. A man who ate like him had no right to such a beautiful body. She pulled her gaze away from him and glanced behind him. A selection of shirts lay scattered on the bed. "Yes, he wants me to—"

"Hey lady, I'm starving!" the other man said.

"Get him dinner," Carissa finished.

She saw Kenric's face change to an expression she'd never seen before. "I'll deal with him," he said in an ominous whisper, storming past her.

She followed behind him with a feeling of dread but decided to return to the kitchen.

∼

KENRIC MARCHED into the living room and found his brother lounging on the couch. "What are you doing here?"

Joshua looked up at him perplexed. "So what happened? I thought I'd come in time to see the hot girl you bought instead I see your mai—"

Kenric covered his mouth and said in a low warning. "Keep your voice down." He removed his hand.

He glanced towards the kitchen where Carissa was. "Why would she care? I'd hope I'd be interrupting something. But just like you...nothing. When are you going to have a little fun?"

Kenric buttoned up his shirt. "What are you doing here?"

"You know I had to see her for myself. Is she on her way?"

"She's already here," he said tucking his shirt in.

Joshua lifted a brow then studied his brother who was straightening his shirt. "Oh, you certainly work fast. Is she in the other room?" A sly grin spread on his face. "Is she getting herself together right now?"

"No. You already met her. She's the one."

"Who's the one?"

"The woman you met at the door."

"She's the one what?"

Kenric rested his hands on his hips, losing patience. "Are you pretending to be this dense to get on my nerves? She's the one I got at the auction."

Joshua jumped to his feet and spun around then grinned as if Kenric had pulled a prank. "No way. That woman—"

Kenric narrowed his eyes and kept his voice even. "I'm serious."

Joshua quickly sobered, realizing his mistake. "Your taste has definitely changed." He headed for the kitchen. "Maybe I didn't get a good look at her."

Kenric grabbed his arm. "And you're not going to."

"No need to be embarrassed. You felt sorry for her, right? Just like I said."

"In two seconds she's going to feel sorry for you."

Joshua frowned. "Why?"

Kenric plastered on a false grin and patted his brother on the cheek. "Because if you don't leave, I'm going to hurt you."

"At least let me get something to eat."

"No."

"Come on—" He stopped when Carissa came out of the kitchen carrying an extra plate of the salmon and rice. Joshua looked at his brother. "Just one bite and I'll leave."

"No."

He poked him in the chest. "If you want to score, I can be your wingman."

Kenric sighed. It was easier to let him stay. "Eat fast."

He hurried over to a chair. "I'm sorry," he said taking Carissa's hand and kissing the back of it. "I didn't realize who you were. I'm Joshua Riverton, Kenric's brother."

"Carissa," she said looking flattered then returning to her seat at the table.

Kenric sat down, annoyed. His brother always had that affect on women. They ate and indulged in light easy chatter, Joshua praising Carissa's culinary skills.

She left to get dessert.

Joshua watched her with interest.

Kenric recognized the look and carefully set his fork down. "She's mine," he said in a low voice.

"Why, because you saw her first? We both know that's not good enough. Why don't we let her decide."

Kenric's tone hardened. He only had one last night with Carissa and he wouldn't let his brother ruin it. "No."

"No?"

"I told you to back off and I mean it. You have Jackie and what's-her-name, Carissa is mine."

Joshua wiped his mouth with his napkin. "I like a challenge." He placed the napkin back on his lap. "And the way she can cook could make any man change his ways."

Carissa returned with an apple crumble scented with cinnamon and topped with whipped cream and chopped pecans.

The two men fell silent as they ate, but tension remained in the air.

"I've never seen two men eat so fast," Carissa said with a nervous laugh once they were through. She stood. "I'll clear the table so you two can—"

Both men stood in unison and said, "Let me help you with the dishes."

"No," she said, looking a little uncomfortable. "That's all right."

"Please, I want to," Kenric said.

And before she could reply, his brother handed him his plate. "Yes, let him take care of the dishes while you rest your feet. I'd love to learn more about you."

It was a smooth move. Kenric silently swore as Joshua

led Carissa away. He stacked the dishes then took them into the kitchen, wanting to break them. It was just like when they were kids. Whatever Kenric had, Joshua had to have it too. Joshua could turn anything into a competition, but Kenric didn't see scoring with Carissa as a game. She meant much more to him than that. But Carissa was a grown woman and he had no claim on her. He couldn't protect her from his brother's charm. Anytime he tried to warn a woman in the past, they just thought he was jealous. Usually he wasn't, but this time he was seething. He turned on the faucet full blast. He was not going to let him win.

"You should go check in on your brother," Carissa said, coming up behind him.

Kenric turned off the faucet and spun around. "Why?"

"He just hurt himself."

Kenric went into the living room and saw his brother on the couch, cradling his wrist, his face in pain. "What happened?"

"I think she broke it," Joshua said.

"What?"

"I was just trying to be friendly and she went all ninja on me. I don't think I'll be able to drive."

"It's just a sprain," Carissa said coming in carrying a first aid kit Kenric didn't even know he had. "You'll be fine."

Joshua looked up at her in fear. "Stay away from me."

She sat down beside him and took his arm. "Stop being a baby. I gave you a warning."

"I didn't hear you," he shot back.

"What did you do?" Kenric asked watching her bandage up his brother's wrist.

"Taught him some manners."

Kenric took out his cell phone and took a picture. "We'll see how long that lasts."

His brother shot him a look then narrowed his gaze and Kenric knew his brother would come up with some sort of revenge. "I need to lie down," he said then got up, went into Kenric's bedroom and closed the door. Kenric almost burst out laughing. His brother lacked imagination, fortunately he didn't. Joshua associated women and pleasure with one place, but Kenric knew he could enjoy Carissa anywhere. And he was determined to squeeze out as much enjoyment that was left in the evening as he could. Kenric assessed his options, wondering how best to play his new advantage, then feigned a weary sigh. "Sorry about that."

Carissa flashed a rueful grin. "You haven't met my sister-in-law."

"What did you do to him?" Kenric said, unable to hide his curiosity.

"I just used a defense move I learned."

"Show me."

She hesitated. "I don't want to hurt you."

He grinned. "That's a first."

She grabbed his arm, twisted it behind him, bent his wrist then let him go. "That's the soft version. I know better than to assault my boss."

He studied her thoughtfully for a moment. "What if I weren't your boss?"

Carissa folded her arms and lowered her gaze. "I

know your brother's a wolf." She lifted her gaze to his. "But I'm not quite sure what you are."

"Let's find out." Kenric tapped his cheek. "Aim for here when you slap me."

"Why would I slap you?"

"Because of this," he said, before sweeping her into his arms and kissing her.

CHAPTER TWELVE

She'd imagined what his lips would taste like, especially after watching him eat. Watching the soft, pink tip of his tongue touch the fullness of his lips as he licked the whipped cream. He definitely was a wolf too and likely could teach his brother a thing or two. His brother was a man she could read easily, but she couldn't read Kenric, which made him a lot more dangerous. Unfortunately, she liked a little danger and she definitely liked him. A man with soft hands and a hard body.

"You're not slapping me yet," he whispered against her mouth.

"Remind me to later."

"I forget easily," he breathed, dropping his mouth to the curve of her neck.

"I don't." She released a soft sigh of pleasure when she felt the tip of his tongue against her skin. "I heard what your brother said."

"About what?"

"About me not being your usual type."

He became still. "Do you want me to give him a black eye?"

She laughed. "No."

"Have him walk with a limp for a while?"

"No, I just wanted you to know you're not my regular type either."

"Good." He kissed her again.

She drew away. "Aren't you going to ask me what my type is?"

"Why would I? All I care about is that I'm your type now."

"I'd better go."

"Yes," he said but didn't release her, placing kisses on her shoulder.

"Do you really want me to slap you?"

"All over if you want," he said in a husky tone.

She drew away and stared at him.

He looked chagrined. "Too much information?"

"No, you just gave me a lot of ideas. Too bad your brother's in the other room."

"I can get rid of him," he said turning.

She grabbed his arm and held him back with a laugh. "No. I really have to go."

He drew her close again. "I wish you didn't."

She gently but firmly held him back. "It's getting late and I have work tomorrow."

He abruptly released her and swore. He stared at her dumbstruck. "Work? I'd forgotten about that."

"Don't worry *boss*," she said stretching the word as she headed for the kitchen. "I didn't."

"How was your date?" Ashley asked Carissa that Monday morning when the two women met in the lobby. She hadn't seen her since she'd run into her when Carissa had been shopping for a dress for the auction.

"It was good."

"Only good?" She looked at her with pity. "Don't worry, you'll meet the right man soon."

Carissa wanted to say she'd already met a man, but of course she couldn't. She still remembered Sara's happy dance when she told her about Kenric's kiss, but she couldn't tell anyone else. No one else could know about her weekend, although it had been one of the best she'd ever had. Just the thought of him made her knees weak.

She stepped into the elevator then turned and saw him. Their eyes met, he nodded in greeting. "Ms. York."

She nodded back. "Mr. Riverton."

They rode the elevator in silence. She was acutely aware of the others around her. She could sense his authority and the tension he brought. She noticed the glances sent his way, the way people tended to part to let him pass. She walked to her office wishing her heart would return to normal. She was at work, she couldn't feel this way about him here.

"Your face is flushed," her assistant said.

She touched her cheek. "It's a hot morning."

"Sure you're not in love?"

"Love?"

"The new clothes, the rosy glow."

"I've just had a busy morning that's all."

Her assistant didn't look convinced, but left her alone. Carissa walked into her office and closed the door. Of course she wasn't in love, she was just a little flustered seeing him again. She took a deep breath. It was nothing. They had just had a nice weekend. He said he wanted to see her again, but what did that mean exactly? What if he just wanted to see her to get free meals? What if she was just a fun novelty?

Her cell phone buzzed. She looked at it and saw a text: Good morning Gorgeous.

She couldn't stop a smile. Morning.

R u alone?

Yes.

She waited for a reply, but nothing happened until he walked through the door, closed it and sat down with a devilish smile on his face. "I found a great place to take you for lunch."

"You can't."

His smile fell. "Why not?"

His crushed expression made her heart leap, he was still interested. *Really* interested, she hadn't dreamt it. "Because you're the boss, remember?" she said, determined to be rational since he wasn't. "Could you imagine the gossip that would spread if people saw us together? I couldn't even tell anyone about this weekend. You're leaving soon, but I have to stay and my reputation will be ruined."

He sighed. "I hadn't thought of that."

"I know."

He lowered his voice and leaned forward, looking like

a mischievous little boy. "It's expensive. I'm sure few people from Simus Labs go there for lunch."

"It's still a risk."

"There's my place. You could—"

"I knew it," she said slapping her desk with false outrage. "You don't want me." She came around the desk and stood in front of him. "You just like the food. You want me to cook you lunches and—"

He laughed. "Yes, you got me. I just want you for your cooking," he said letting his gaze slide down her body in a slow, sensuous study.

Carissa cleared her throat. "My eyes are up here."

Kenric kept his gaze focused on her legs, showing the same intent of a hungry lion spotting a gazelle. "I know where your eyes are."

She returned to sit behind her desk. "You're worse than your brother."

His eyes met hers. "Only when it comes to you."

She swallowed. "We cannot do this."

"There's a restaurant near my apartment. No one from Simus Labs goes there. It's not far and no one will be paying attention with us leaving separately."

Carissa bit her lip. The idea was tempting. No, *he* was tempting. "I don't know."

"Don't you trust me?"

"I'm not sure I trust myself."

"I'll make sure no one knows about us."

She was taking a risk, but she didn't care. "Okay, it's a date."

～

CARISSA SPENT the next week in heaven. Her secret lunches with Kenric were the highlight of her day. At the office, they could communicate without words, just a look or a nod from him made a jolt of delight course through her.

During a department head meeting, she couldn't keep her eyes off him, but this time she didn't see a hatchet man, instead she imagined him with his shirt off, which definitely wasn't professional. When she saw the senior VP, Nathan Cole, send her an odd look, she straightened in her seat and returned her thoughts to the topic of the meeting. Nobody could know what was happening between them.

Nathan came into her office. He was a slick man with commercial white teeth, who'd once tried to block Carissa's promotion due to her lack of a college degree. Although she'd won him over, she didn't trust him. "Riverton's definitely a hardass," he said taking a seat. "Not sure there will be much left after they've finished cutting us up."

"At least those of us left don't have to worry about losing our jobs," she said. "It's basic restructuring."

"Are you actually starting to believe that BS? You think that talking puppet really knows what Barra Industries is planning for us? Do you actually think he gives a damn? Don't be naïve."

"I don't think he's hiding anything. I think he's been forthcoming and truthful."

Nathan flashed an ugly smile. "So is that how you're going to play it? You're going to swallow whatever he shoves at you because of a crush?"

"You're way out of line."

"Am I? One moment you're talking to Wexler about how much you hate him...oh, you think I didn't hear that? And the next you're defending him like he's our savior."

"Don't exaggerate. I may not like everything he says or does, but I respect him as a professional."

He shrugged. "Hey, I don't fault you. If I had an advantage I'd try to use it too."

"Advantage?"

"He's a straight guy and you're a woman. You want to keep your job so—" He winked at her. "You want the boss to like you."

"I am not trying to—"

"Come on York. It's obvious. Everyone's noticed your new look and attitude. And you look great, there's no denying that. If I weren't a married man—" He stopped when Carissa shook her head, sending him a warning stare. "I'm here because I want to give you some advice. Give up. You're wasting your time with Riverton, so stop embarrassing yourself."

Carissa felt like falling through the floor in humiliation—people thought what she had was a one-sided crush?—but she managed to keep her eyes and voice steady. "I am not going after Riverton to keep my job. And I don't want to hear you say that again."

He stood, resting a hand on his chest. "I'm not the enemy here. I'm only trying to help you keep your dignity. I've noticed how you've looked at Riverton and I'm not the only one. Make sure he doesn't notice or you'll get hurt. You're not used to men like him. The truth is, he's a cold son of a bitch who'd never give you the time of day." He turned and walked out the door.

Once he left, Carissa buried her face in her hands, her cheeks burning. *He does like me!* she wanted to say. Did they really think she'd changed her look just to get his attention? For the last several days, she'd felt attractive and confident and now she realized everyone just saw her as a pathetic woman pining after her boss. Was she being that obvious? She didn't think she was. Did they think so low of her that they couldn't accept that a new look meant she felt better about herself? Maybe she should stop. He'd be leaving in a couple of months anyway and she wasn't keeping their relationship secret very well. It didn't even feel like their secret anymore with people not believing he'd ever be interested in her. He played his role well. No one suspected there was any interest on his side.

Carissa rested her head on her desk and groaned. She'd worked hard to build her reputation and in just a few weeks she'd put it in jeopardy.

Someone knocked on the door.

She lifted her head off her desk, straightened her hair and said in a bright voice, "Come in,"

Kenric entered.

She jumped to her feet and said in a rush. "You shouldn't be here."

He looked at her startled. "Why not? I came for the employee files we discussed in the meeting."

"Oh yes, right. Sorry." She sat back down, typed some information into her computer. "I just sent you soft-copies." She rushed over to her metal file cabinet, searched through it and pulled out several manila files. "And here are the hardcopies," she said handing them to him.

"Thank you. You seem...rushed."

"I just don't want to waste your time."

"You'd never do that." He stepped closer and lowered his voice. "I'll have to reschedule lunch."

"That's okay. I don't think we should see each other anymore."

"What?"

"It's been fun but—"

His gaze sharpened. "What happened? Did someone find out?"

"Sort of."

"Who?"

She moved away from him, being near him was too distracting. "It's nobody's fault." She sat down behind her desk, grateful for the barrier. "I'm the problem. I haven't been able to play our relationship as cool as you and others are starting to notice. People are talking. It's a pride thing for me," she said embarrassed. "Nobody can believe that a man like you would be interested in me."

He frowned, confused. "Why not?"

"Remember what your brother said?"

His tone hardened. "Don't bring my brother into this."

"It's silly really," she said forcing a laugh. "I mean, what are we doing anyway? You'll soon be gone and I'll be the pathetic HR dirrector who'd lusted after her boss. After a couple months I'll get my reputation back and—"

Kenric rested his fists on the desk and leaned forward. "Do you want me to make it formal?"

"Formal?"

"Yes, do you want me to take you out publicly?"

"No, that will be worse." She looked up at him, fear on her face.

He looked at her stunned. "How could it be worse?"

"Then they'll *really* think I'm desperate to keep my job."

"What's wrong with this place? What's wrong with a man being interested in an attractive woman? I've looked at the legal stipulations and there's nothing against us dating. And although I am the boss, I'm only here temporarily so I won't be your boss for long. I've know guys who've dated their employees and—"

Carissa didn't allow herself to dwell on the compliment. "It's different here. I told you, right now is a delicate time and the rumors are the fiercest when people are tense and unsure. I have to live here, you don't. Please."

Kenric rubbed his chin. "I don't like this."

She sighed resigned. "I know. So we have to stop."

"I don't want to stop. So what's your other plan?"

She paused. She hadn't expected him to fight her. He was a reasonable and rational man. They were having fun, but she knew it wasn't meant to last. "I didn't think I needed one."

His phone rang. He looked at it. "I have to get this." He looked at her. "This discussion isn't over. I'll call you."

"Promise you won't say anything to anyone until you talk to me," she said.

He opened the door and answered the phone. "River-ton," he said before leaving.

She should have known not to try for a promise. He wasn't the type. But she hoped with time he'd see her side. What were they doing? The relationship wasn't going to go anywhere. Why try to hide something that wouldn't last?

Exactly, because it wouldn't last, her mind said. Who cared what anyone else thought if she was having the time of her life? Who cared what they said behind her back as long as she was happy? Was she really ready to throw it all away because of what Nathan said? She didn't respect him that much and being with Kenric was wonderful.

Was it so wrong to wish that she could show him off a bit? To be able to say 'He's with me'? Sure, her desire stemmed from her pride, but wasn't she allowed a little of it?

"Uh, oh. What did you do?" Sara asked when she stopped by to check on Carissa.

Carissa left her front door open for her to pass then went and sat on the couch. "I'm not seeing Kenric anymore."

Sara sat beside her. "Why?"

"Because I can't do it. I'm all wrong for this. There are just too many secrets in my life right now. I can't tell anyone why I'm wearing new clothes because of the

Black Stockings Society and I can't tell anyone I'm seeing this great guy."

"Why do you feel you have to explain yourself anyway?"

"What?"

"Even if you weren't following some instructions from the club, if you wanted to wear new stockings or change your hair or buy a new car you can do it without telling anyone. Why do they matter? Who are they? Are they important?"

"No, but—"

"And would you really drop a great guy because of what other people may or may not be thinking about you?"

"He'll be leaving in a couple of months."

"And that will be even better, then you won't have to hide anymore. Carissa, it's time to live your life on your terms. You don't have to prove or explain anything. Besides, people will talk anyway."

"I guess I'm a little afraid because he's good at this. Too good. What if I'm not the only one? What if he's seeing someone else? Hell, he could be charming half the woman at the office and I'd never know."

Sara poked her in the arm. "You know he's not."

"I'd never know anything with the mask he wears."

"Do you really want to break up or are you finding excuses?"

"I told you, I'm scared."

"Of what?"

"Of really falling for him."

Sara looked at Carissa with pity. "Don't you know you already have?"

Carissa covered her face. "Isn't it awful?"

"No, be honest with him and see where this leads." She clapped her hands together. "Unfortunately, I can't stay long. I came by to check on your progress with your next assignment." She opened her cell phone then scrolled through a document. "It's time for phase two."

"Phase two?"

"Yes, dinner with the family."

Carissa shook her head. "No way."

Sara nodded then tapped the image on her cell phone screen. "It's part of your instructions. Just with your brother and sister-in-law, not your entire family."

"No. Absolutely not."

"This is the perfect two way approach. You will either find out how serious he is, or you'll scare him away. You wanted someone who wasn't ashamed of you, right?"

Carissa sighed. Kenric already knew she'd been married twice, if meeting her family made him run, then it was for the best. "Yes."

"Good." Sara pointed to an image on the screen. "And you're going to wear these."

CHAPTER THIRTEEN

Dinner. She'd invited him to have dinner with her family. He was glad she'd changed her mind about them not seeing each other, but he was still surprised by the request. He knocked on the door to her apartment.

Carissa opened it then held up her hand. "Don't say anything, I know I look ridiculous. A friend had this crazy idea—"

"That I like very much," he said, letting his gaze appreciate her silk red blouse, pencil thin black leather skirt and stripped patterned dark stockings. He kissed her then handed her the colorful mixed bouquet he'd bought. "You look wonderful."

She took the bouquet suddenly looking shy. "Thank you," she said, then quickly grabbed a vase and hurried into the kitchen. "But you're early. Everything's not ready yet."

He followed her into the kitchen. "I thought I could help you."

She fell silent for a moment, filling the sink with some tepid water then resting the stems of the bouquet inside before she started to cut the ends. "You don't have to do anything," she finally said.

Kenric studied her face. She had that odd rushed look again. "Is something wrong?"

"No. Please sit down. Do you want anything to drink?"

"No, I told you, I came early to help."

"Can you chop?" She put the flowers in the vase and added the plant food that came in the small package.

"Nope."

"Slice?"

"No."

"Then how did you expect to help?" she asked with a note of frustration.

He smiled. "I can set a table to military precision."

She pointed to a cupboard, her tone softening. "The dishes are over there." She pointed to a drawer. "And the utensils."

Kenric set to work then after he was finished he stood and watched her. There was a tense energy he couldn't understand. "So your brother's name is Glenn," he said resting against the counter.

"Yes and his wife's Lina and they're expecting a boy next month."

Kenric nodded. "Are you afraid they won't like me?"

Carissa spun around surprised. "No. It's just..."

"What?" He pressed when she fell silent again.

"You might find out a lot more about me than you want to know."

"I want to know everything."

"You may get your wish," she said but she didn't sound happy.

She was surviving this, Carissa thought as she watched everyone eat. She'd survived Lina pointing to Carissa's stockings and comparing her legs to a zebra, and even Glenn's strange response to Kenric when he first met him. Instead of the jovial handshake, which he usually greeted strangers with, his smile froze on his face and he stared at Kenric for a second longer than normal, before recovering himself. Kenric appeared disturbed by his response, but to her relief let it pass and now they were on the main course and nothing disastrous had happened. There had been some awkward pauses, especially when Kenric admitted that the two of them had met at work, but weren't telling anyone about their relationship until later, but overall, the conversation flowed smoothly.

"Another masterpiece," Kenric said setting his fork down. "She keeps me coming back for more."

Lina giggled. "Be careful. Carissa might try to persuade you to be her third husband."

Carissa shot her a glance and Glenn nudged her in warning.

Kenric only grinned. "She won't have to try hard."

Carissa stood, feeling both flattered and embarrassed at the same time. "Let me check on dessert."

"I'll help you," Glenn said. Once they were alone in

the kitchen he said, "Where did you say you met this guy?"

"At work, like he said. He's my new boss, that's why we're keeping our relationship quiet for now." She took out the lemon meringue pie.

Glenn took out the dessert forks and dishes. "Are you sure you can trust him?"

Carissa looked at her brother surprised by his tense tone. "If you have questions, you should be asking him not me."

He leaned against the counter. "I just think you're rebounding too fast after Morris. You should give yourself some time."

"What don't you like about him?"

Glenn frowned. "I didn't say I didn't like him."

"He makes me happy and I like being with him." She paused then said, "What was that look between you two?"

"What look?" he said, suddenly avoiding her gaze.

She lifted his chin, forcing him to face her. "You had an odd expression on your face when you first saw him."

"He's just not what I expected for you."

"I know he looks mean."

The sound of Lina's laughter drifted towards them.

"And as you can see, he's very social," Carissa finished.

"Hmm."

"Try to give him a chance." *Heaven knows I've given Lina plenty of them.*

"It's just we got used to Morris—"

"Morris is gone and you weren't that close anyway."

"I mean..." He pulled on his ear, looking awkward. "Don't you think you're reaching a little out of your depth? Morris was quite a stretch, but this guy is on a whole new level."

"And you don't think I deserve him?"

He shook his head. "I didn't mean that. Just that guys like him are a little savvier than you're used to. Be careful."

"I am." She picked up the pie and headed to the dining room, but something about his warning worried her.

CHAPTER FOURTEEN

"I don't like it," Lina said, returning to their apartment with a scowl. She sat on the couch and folded her arms. "Not one bit."

"You sounded like you were having a blast," Glenn said closing the door behind them.

"I was raised to be polite. But I still don't like it."

He sat beside her. "What's not to like?"

"He's not from here. What if he convinces Carissa to leave? What will happen to us?"

"We'll be fine."

"At least Morris has ties here. We don't know anything about his family."

"We know that he's rich, I thought that would make you happy."

She glared at him. "Are you saying that I only think about money?"

He tenderly brushed his knuckles against her cheek. "I was just teasing, honey."

She pushed his hand away. "I'm serious."

"Carissa has a right to her own life. I thought you wanted her to be happy."

"I do, but something's not right. Something's bothering me and I don't know what. We're going to have to keep an eye on them."

"Hmm," Glenn said trying to sound noncommittal. "I've got something I have to do," he said then left, before she could complain. He went into his study and closed the door then sat behind his desk and swore. He was just as concerned as his wife, but for completely different reasons. Riverton was dangerous. He knew, because he'd met him before. He couldn't afford Riverton remembering that meeting, however. So far, there hadn't been any recognition on his part and maybe he never would—fifteen years was a long time—but he didn't like dealing with maybes. He liked to know for sure. He swore, his sister seemed so happy and he didn't want to ruin that for her, but he had a lot more on the line than she did. She hadn't known Riverton for long so maybe it wouldn't last.

He opened a drawer and took out the second cell phone his wife didn't know about then made a call. "I need you to look into someone for me."

HE HAD this strange feeling of dread that he couldn't shake. Kenric stood in the kitchen washing dishes, although he could stack the dishwasher he found the task oddly relaxing. He kept going over the dinner in his mind. There was something familiar about Glenn. Why did he feel as if he'd met him somewhere before? Where could they have met? They certainly didn't travel in the same circles and Glenn was years younger than him, but something bothered him. Maybe he was confusing him with someone else. That had to be it, but somehow he knew that was wrong. They had a history.

"You didn't like them," Carissa said coming into the kitchen.

He focused back on the dishes. "Why do you say that?"

"You have your henchman look."

"Henchman?"

"Never mind,' she said with chagrin.

He grabbed her arm. "No, tell me."

"Ew...you're getting me all wet."

He looked down at his wet hands. "Oh sorry," he said releasing her.

"If you're determined to keep washing dishes, I'll have to pick up some plastic gloves for you."

He lifted a brow. "You're changing the subject. What do you mean by 'henchman'?"

"When I first saw you, you reminded me of a hench-man. Cold, distant and ready to perform your orders in a swift efficient manner."

He winced. "Well, that's not very flattering."

Carissa wrapped her arms around his waist. "Fortu-nately, you changed my mind, but sometimes I still see that look, like now. What are you thinking? What didn't you like?"

"Nothing, I had a good time and the food was

wonderful. I'm not sure they warmed to me, but I'm used to that."

"Is it me?" She let him go and looked at his profile. "Did Lina's comment bother you?"

He frowned. "What comment?"

"About me wanting a third husband."

"Oh that."

"Well..." Carissa pressed when he didn't continue.

"I meant what I said." He set the dishes aside to dry. "What are we going to do about work?"

"I'll ignore the rumors."

"I think we should put an end to them."

"And I told you, there's no need to, you'll be gone in a few months anyway."

He turned from the sink and dried his hands. "I wish you'd stop saying that. If I have to commute I will. I plan to stick around."

"Oh."

"You sound surprised."

"I am."

"What part of 'you don't have to try hard to make me your third husband,' don't you understand?"

"I thought you were just helping me save face."

"There's no one else around except us and I'm still saying it. I thought I made it clear that I like being with you. Maybe I haven't been very convincing." He pulled her close and kissed her then looked down at her clothes. "Too bad you're not wearing an apron."

"Why?"

"Because in my dreams I was always taking it off you."

"Really?"

"Yes." He leaned in to kiss her but she held him away. "What?" he asked.

"I just got an idea."

"But—"

"Go into the living room. I'll be right there. There was always a fantasy I wanted to play out with my third husband."

His eyes lit with interest. "Really?"

"Yes, are you willing to help me?"

"Okay, but what do I have to do?"

"Just go into the living room."

"That's it?"

"You'll like this. I promise. When you get there, close your eyes."

He sighed then did.

"Okay, they're closed," he said.

Moments later he heard her heels on the floor then felt her presence in front of him. "Hey stranger, do you come here often?" she said.

He opened his eyes and saw Carissa holding a tray of strawberries and chocolate wearing only high heels and an apron.

"Is this your first time here?" she continued.

He stared up at her open-mouthed. "What?"

"You're supposed to play along. I'm your waitress and—"

He jumped to his feet and removed his shirt and trousers with an efficient speed that shocked her. "I'm not hungry," he said in a low voice then pulled her into his arms.

"This isn't part of the fantasy," Carissa said, her voice breathless as she felt the heat of his skin against hers. "You're supposed to nibble on the strawberries and—"

His hungry dark gaze slid down the length of her. "Who wants to nibble on a little piece of fruit," he said, his hands scaling down her bare back to her waist, sending a warm shiver through her. "When they've got a big piece of chocolate?" He didn't expect a reply and he didn't get one when he captured her mouth with his own in a kiss that was hard, hot and searching. Within seconds he changed her fantasy into something more exciting and definitely wilder. Because she liked watching him eat, and found it subtlety erotic, she'd imagined stripping off his shirt, pressing her body against his while feeding him fresh strawberries dipped in chocolate. His beautiful mouth wet from the sweet juice and stained with a hint of red, which she'd kiss away.

Instead, his mouth devoured hers with an appetite more ravenous than she could have dreamed. His lips covered hers with a passionate fury that made her forget herself and all her insecurities. She'd been a little worried that she may have gone too far. She'd once tried a fantasy with Morris—she'd pretended to be a police officer who'd pulled him over for speeding—but the effort had fallen flat when he found her outfit ridiculous and the dialogue more so, reminding her that 'people like us' don't do 'things like that'. The incident had left them both embarrassed and she'd never tried to surprise him again.

But not Kenric. He made her feel as if she were as desirous as a Bond Girl and as sultry as a beautiful stage star. She didn't even realize he'd removed her apron until she lay naked on the couch, his hot flesh covering hers.

He reached for a strawberry and traced the shape of her mouth with its tip. "You're so beautiful."

That's when the tears fell. She didn't even know she was crying until she saw his face suddenly change.

He started to get up. "Am I hurting you?"

Carissa grabbed his arm, nearly frantic, pulling him back down, scared to ruin the mood. "No, please don't stop."

He brushed away a tear. "But—"

"I'm so happy." She kissed him. "You've made me so happy."

She felt his tension ebb and his face relaxed into a devious grin. "I haven't even done anything yet."

"Then why are you making me wait?"

He held the strawberry over her mouth. "Open wide."

She did just that, but instead of the strawberry he gave her his tongue instead, which she didn't mind. It explored her mouth then slid a sensuous path down her neck, then to her chest where he captured her breast in his mouth, his tongue toying with her nipple, then he licked her sweet center until she felt she was in a whirl-wind of ecstasy. He followed soon after, his entry as smooth as hot butter melting on a warm biscuit. She wrapped her legs around him, wanting to drive him in deeper never wanting the sensation to end. She'd always thought that 'two becoming one' was just a myth until that moment. She felt bonded to him, not just on a physical level, but something much deeper. Deeper than she'd ever felt with another man.

For a brief moment she wanted to push him away, to reclaim herself, but then she surrendered, knowing her heart was already his. Knowing that Lina was right, he'd have to be careful because she had every intention of making him hers. "Do you think husband number three will like my fantasy?" she whispered in his ear.

He grinned then gave her a reply that needed no words.

HUSBAND NUMBER THREE. Kenric lay on the couch holding Carissa, his body languid, his mind never more alive. *Husband number three.* Other men may be daunted by the idea, but he liked the challenge. The other two didn't know what they'd lost. He hadn't even considered getting married for another few years, but she'd changed all that. She'd changed a lot of things. He couldn't imagine a future without her in it. *Husband number three.* Three had always been a lucky number for him. The prospect didn't bother him, his family would be a problem, but he'd handle them. For the first time in his life nothing felt impossible.

OVER THE NEXT several weeks they expanded meetings from private lunches and intimate dinners to include romantic breakfasts. When Carissa caught Kenric reaching for the cinnamon to add to one of her recipes, before changing his mind and putting it back, she decided it was time to buy him an apron and have him help in the kitchen.

She gave him the apron one Saturday afternoon when he stopped by her place. She'd given him the gift after he'd taken a seat on the couch and he'd received it with the same awe as if she'd bought him an expensive watch or a new car. He gingerly pulled the apron out of the bag then ran his hand over it like he was skimming over silk instead of rough cotton.

"This is really mine?" he asked, inspecting the pocket and then the trim.

Carissa tried not to laugh, not understanding why he was so impressed by such a simple gift. "Yes. Now you can really help me in the kitchen."

His gaze met hers, his eyes bright with eagerness. "I get to help you in the kitchen? I won't be in the way?"

"No, I like your help," she said, but from the expression on his face she might as well have said 'you've just won the lottery'.

He jumped to his feet and put it on. "Tell me what you want me to do."

"I hadn't planned on anything special."

"I don't care."

And she soon discovered he meant what he said. No task was too menial, whether it was scrubbing potatoes, peeling oranges or washing lettuce. He never complained, always following her lead, which surprised her. He also liked offering suggestions that never failed to make whatever dish she was making more delicious.

Twice they had Malcolm join them—Carissa didn't want him to feel neglected—and they baked poppy seed cookies and made a lemon cake and once, all three of them went to the beach and had a picnic.

"I'm not sure I can keep our relationship a secret much longer," Kenric said one afternoon as they lazed on the couch after they'd returned from shopping at a Farmer's Market.

"We just have another month to go," Carissa said.

"Exactly," he said with a heavy sigh. "But it feels like years."

"Why should anyone know?"

"Because I want to show you off. Sneaking around like this makes what we have feel dirty somehow. Like we're doing something wrong."

His words pleased her but she knew she had to be rational. "The overall mood at work is still too delicate."

"What's delicate about it? I've been here over a month, the restructuring is going along smoothly. No one else is getting laid off."

"People still feel a little displaced even though there haven't been any more layoffs. There's still departments being shifted and changes that people have to grow accustomed to. That takes time for people to get adjusted to."

"What does that have to do with us?"

"It just doesn't look good. I have to appear to be neutral. How will anyone feel they can trust me, if they know I'm seeing you?"

"So I'm still the enemy."

"Try to see it from another point of view."

"I don't want to," he said in a petulant voice.

She looped her arm through his and rested her head on his shoulder. "What if I make you—"

He shook his head. "It won't work."

"But you haven't tasted it yet."

"It still won't work." He gazed down at her. "We're just delaying the inevitable."

"Please just consider my reputation. People have already said—"

He stiffened. "People have already said what?"

"You're getting upset."

"I'm not upset. Tell me what people have said. And who are they?"

"Forget it. Let's just wait a couple more weeks and then we can decide how we want to announce our relationship. Okay?"

Before he could reply her cell phone alerted her to a text. She looked at it then swore and jumped to her feet.

"What is it?"

Carissa put on her shoes. "We have to go. It's Lina."

"Is she okay?"

"She said her water broke."

CHAPTER FIFTEEN

Carissa dialed her brother's cell as she raced up the stairs, but it kept going to voicemail. She'd told him that he didn't have the luxury of turning off his phone, especially with Lina so close to her due date. She imagined Lina alone and writhing in pain.

She pounded on the door, but when she didn't get a quick reply, she took out her spare key and opened it. She rushed inside and saw water on the floor. She knew a woman's water broke, but she'd never expected this much. She frantically searched the apartment.

"Lina! Lina, we're here," she said, rushing towards the bedroom.

"Oh thank goodness you're here," Lina said coming out of the kitchen.

"Have you called Glenn? How close are the contractions?"

"Contractions?"

Carissa paused. "Aren't you in labor?"

"No, this place is flooded because one of the kitchen pipes burst or something."

Carissa blinked, nonplussed. "A kitchen pipe?"

"Yes."

Carissa held up her cell phone and waved the text at her. "You said 'my water broke'."

"And it did, in the kitchen."

"What did I tell you about sending me messages like this! I said emergencies only."

"This is an emergency! Don't you see the water? It's everywhere."

"You could have called a plumber instead of calling us up here."

She lifted a sly brow. "Oooh, did I interrupt you two doing something kinky?"

"It's not funny."

"Oh, that's right," Lina said dismissively. "You don't do things like that."

"I'm furious with you." She turned to Kenric. "I'm sorry about dragging you into this."

"Why are you apologizing?" Lina demanded. "I did—do need your help."

Carissa made a sweeping gesture with her arms. "That's it. This is the last time I'm going to respond to your crazy texts and I mean it."

"Want me to look at it?" Kenric asked.

Lina laughed. "Men with hands like yours wouldn't know a wrench from a washer."

"Lina," Carissa said in warning.

Kenric shrugged without offense. "She's right, but I'll

still take a look anyway." He started towards the kitchen then halted at the sight of a photo on the bookshelf.

"That's Glenn," Lina said noticing his interest. "He was attending college at the time. That's him on campus. Handsome isn't he?"

Kenric didn't respond, almost as if he hadn't heard her then headed to the kitchen. Carissa wanted to ask him about his strange response but Lina spoke first.

"I hope he doesn't make things worse," she said.

Carissa went to the closet and grabbed a mop. "I don't think that's possible."

"I don't know why you're so angry. How was I supposed to know you'd misinterpret—"

"Don't call me again. I mean it. I'm through with your games."

"It's not a game."

"You know very well you could have handled this on your own."

She spread her arms out wide. "Look at me. I've got the belly the size of a beach ball. I can hardly reach my top shelf anymore."

"You're not helpless, you just like to act like it," Carissa said then started to mop up the water.

"I think I found the problem," Kenric said coming into the room minutes later. "But your husband should check things out before you call in a plumber. I'm not sure you'd want the expense."

"My husband can afford whatever we need."

Carissa stiffened at her tone. "That's not what—"

"It's okay," Kenric said.

"I'm really sorry about that," Carissa said as she unlocked the door to her apartment. When Kenric didn't respond she turned to him nervous. Was he angry? But his expression didn't look angry. He looked pale. She gently touched his sleeve, concerned. "Kenric?"

He looked at her as if coming out of a deep thought. "Hmm?"

"What's wrong? Are you sick?"

He shook his head. "Nothing. No, I'm fine."

She didn't believe him. She touched his forehead. "You're not running a fever, but you may want to lie down. I'm really sorry about this."

"You don't have to be. Family is family, right?"

But she didn't care for his nonchalant tone, something about it didn't ring true.

"But something is bothering you."

He sighed and rubbed the back of his neck. "I don't know much about plumbing so it might not be anything."

"What?"

"The pipe didn't burst, it was loosened. It may have become loose over time, but—"

"But you think that she might have done it deliberately."

"No, I don't know. I don't see why she would." He swallowed and rubbed the back of his neck again. "Excuse me," he said then left her and went down the hall.

Carissa heard the bathroom door close and swore,

hoping he was okay. Lina had been up to one of her tricks again, but she vowed she wouldn't fall for it again.

HE WASN'T GOING *to be sick*. Kenric took several deep gulps of air until he felt his stomach settle. He gripped the side of the basin, until the wave of nausea passed then he splashed his face with cold water. He'd lied to Carissa and he didn't like the feeling. He had been disturbed by what he'd suspected Lina had done to the pipe, but that wasn't what had bothered him. It was Glenn's picture. Now he knew where he'd remembered him from and why. The why was the worst part. He took another gulp of air as another wave of nausea hit. He squeezed his eyes shut and gripped his hands into fists. No, he could control this. He would manage. The sensation passed and he splashed his face with more cold water. He wouldn't let that bastard win. Carissa was the greatest thing ever to come into his life and he wouldn't lose her.

Kenric stared at his reflection in the mirror, suddenly feeling as helpless as he had fifteen years ago. Why did he have to be Carissa's brother? He'd never thought he'd meet him again, now as he remembered the dinner soon the sound of his voice and his mannerism came flooding back to him.

He should end their relationship. It was the best way out, no matter how much it hurt. He should cut things clean and quick and never look back.

He heard a soft knock on the door. "Kenric? Kenric, are you alright?"

The sound of her soft voice pierced his very soul. He loved her. It wasn't until this moment that he realized how much. "I'm fine," he said wiping away tears as regrets assailed him.

"Are you sure?"

"Yea. I'll be out in a minute." He heard her hesitate, then leave. He stared at his reflection again, suddenly feeling as tired as an old man. The face looking back at him said, *You should let her go.*

I don't want to, he replied.

This is bigger than you. What if she finds out?

She doesn't have to find out yet and her brother hasn't said anything.

You know he will and what will you do when he tells her who gave him the scar that nearly killed him?

Kenric put the face towel back. Letting her go was the wisest choice, a noble one. It would be best for both of them. He opened the door, feeling drained and defeated, suddenly he felt her arms around him as she hugged him close. "Don't worry, I'll take care of you."

At first he didn't move, too stunned to respond. She'd been waiting there for him? He gathered her close, knowing he wasn't going to be wise and he didn't care about being noble. He had her and he wasn't going to let her go.

CHAPTER SIXTEEN

Joshua hated having surprise visitors, especially at night. Especially this late at night. He glanced at the clock and said a few choice words. He made sure to juggle his women so that they never ran into each other and he'd trained each one not to appear on his doorstep unannounced. So he was very annoyed when his doorbell rang close to eleven o'clock. He glanced at the beautiful woman by his side, who looked as annoyed as he felt. "Don't worry, I'll get rid of whoever it is."

"You'd better make it quick," she purred, rubbing her foot down his leg.

He grabbed his robe and winked. "You won't even know I'm gone." He rushed to the door then swore when he saw his brother, but all words of anger died on his lips when he saw his face.

Fear gripped his heart. "What happened?"

Kenric avoided his gaze. When he spoke his voice was barely a whisper. "I met him again."

He didn't need to elaborate. They both knew who 'he' was. They'd never dignify him with a name. The fact that he was human was bad enough. "Are you sure it was him?"

He nodded.

"Josh?" a female voice called from the hallway.

"Not now," he said.

Kenric stiffened. "Damn, I'm sorry. I should have realized you'd have company." He forced a smile. "A single man has rules, right?"

Joshua didn't care about getting laid right now, all he cared about was the look on his brother's face. "She can keep." He turned to her. "I've got some business, keep yourself occupied."

She made a face then returned to the bedroom.

Kenric ran a tired hand down his face. "I've been avoiding Carissa for two days, but I shouldn't have come here."

"I'm glad you did," Joshua said leading his brother over to a seat. He poured a drink then handed him the glass. Kenric absently took it, but didn't raise it to his lips.

Joshua took a long swallow then sat in front of him, feeling both frightened and angry. One moment feeling like a kid again; the next, like a man who wanted revenge. "When did you see him? Where? How?"

"Just recently." Kenric laughed without humor. "I actually had dinner with him and his wife."

"The bastard's married?"

"Expecting a kid too."

"Are you kidding me?"

"I wish I were." Kenric looked down at the glass then mumbled, "He's Carissa's brother."

Joshua leaned in closer, sure he'd misunderstood. "What? It sounded like you said he's Carissa's brother."

Kenric nodded. "Yes, that's what I said.

He swore.

Kenric nodded again. "Exactly."

Joshua slapped his leg. "I knew it! The moment she nearly broke my wrist I should have known Miss Crazy was bad news."

"She's not crazy," Kenric said in a quiet voice.

Joshua decided now wasn't the time to tease him. "So how are you going to dump her? Do you need me to give you some tips?"

Kenric set the glass aside. "I'm not going to dump her."

"You may not want to," Joshua said, choosing his words carefully. "But you have to. You can't see her again. It will hurt less if you make it clean and quick. You kick her sweet ass to the curb and find something sweeter to warm your bed. Kenric?" he said when his brother remained silent and kept his gaze focused on the ground.

"I heard you," he said in a too soft tone.

"But that doesn't mean you're listening. I don't care how you feel about her right now. It will pass. You can't be connected with a guy like that."

He closed his eyes. "I know."

"So stop things now."

He rested his head back. "I can't."

"Of course you can," Joshua said hating the look of defeat on his brother's face. "You had your little fun with her now leave. It's not like she can track you down. Even if she did, she has no claim on you."

"I know." He shook his head. "But I can't."

"Kenric, she's nobody."

Kenric's gaze sharpened as did his tone. "She's somebody to me."

"I don't know what her hold is over you, but she'll ruin your life. That's your problem. You get serious too fast. You'll be bringing in a whole lot of heartache that isn't worth it."

"She's not part of what happened."

"How do you know? You said she's his older sister right? You think she's completely ignorant of his past? Do you think she didn't know what he was up to?"

"No, she didn't know her ex was dealing drugs either."

Joshua's voice cracked in surprise. "She has an ex who's a dealer?"

"Was."

"Is he dead?"

"He's in jail."

Joshua stared at his brother stunned. "And you believe her? Are you really that naïve? Is her flesh so sweet that you've lost your mind? I mean, the way you're defending her you'd think you were ready to marry her."

When his brother didn't reply, he swore fiercely and stood. "You can sleep with her all you want, but you can't do that."

Kenric lifted his drink and took a long swallow then said, "Why not?"

"Do you really want to tie your life to a woman like that?"

He set the glass down and kept his gaze lowered.

"Because the moment you put a ring on her finger," Joshua continued. "You lose me as a brother."

Kenric met his gaze. "Is that a threat?"

Joshua stared back. "It's a promise."

HE'D BEEN ACTING strange the last several days. At first she'd thought he was coming down with something, then he'd told her he was busy and she hadn't seen him for two days, except for brief sightings at work. Then yesterday he knocked on her front door holding a beautiful set of diamond earrings, said he missed her and then made love to her as if he'd been away for years. She couldn't complain, but she didn't understand him. For a moment she'd been worried that Lina's fiasco had made him change his mind about her, or maybe teasing him about becoming her third husband was no longer funny. But now he seemed more resolved than ever to be a couple, even talking about their future together.

Carissa looked over at Kenric as he slept. Aside from his odd behavior, he also had a very strange habit of sleeping *underneath* the pillow.

"How come every time I wake up I find your head under the pillow?" she asked the next morning as they prepared to eat breakfast. She grinned. "Do I snore or something?"

Kenric poured orange juice into two glasses, a soft smile touching his lips.

Carissa stared at him horrified. "I do not snore!"

He put the carton of orange juice away and carried the glasses to the table. "Yes, you do."

"No one has ever told me I snore."

"They were being polite," he said taking a seat. "This looks great," he said looking at the fresh fruit and pancakes.

"Well, maybe you shouldn't spend the night anymore, if sleeping over is so awful for you."

"Don't worry, I've already thought of a solution. I'm getting earplugs."

She sat down and grabbed the plate of pancakes before he could reach them. "I don't snore so loud that you need—"

He reached for his phone. "Do you want proof?"

Carissa blinked and set the plate down. "You recorded me?"

"I thought you looked cute. You only do it when you're lying on your back."

"I sleep on my side."

"You start on your side, but usually end up on your back and then it's..." He held his head back and made loud snoring sounds.

Carissa folded her arms. "I do not sound like that."

Kenric laughed and grabbed his phone. "I'm being nice. Do you really want to see?"

She jumped up and snatched it from him. "No, and isn't that invasion of privacy?"

"I'm not posting it on the web, I just wanted evidence."

She set the phone down. "I think you're making it up to annoy me." She narrowed her eyes and pointed at him. "Maybe you put your head under the pillow because you're afraid of the dark and you don't want to admit it."

He nodded looking serious. "I am afraid of the dark, especially when it sounds like I'm sleeping next to a giant grizzly bear."

"A statement like that and you'll get your home cooked meals privileges revoked."

Kenric rested his chin in his hand, closed his eyes and made more snoring sounds.

"I mean it," Carissa said embarrassed, but unable to stop a laugh at his ridiculous impression.

His snoring impression grew louder.

She crunched up a napkin and threw it at him. "You're an idiot."

He laughed and picked up his fork. "Okay, I'll stop teasing you. You're right. You don't snore—"

"I knew it."

"That loud," he finished, then winked at her.

THE FOLLOWING DAY Carissa went to the convenience store to find snoring remedies and was in the health aisle looking at breathing strips when she saw Lina. She ducked, hoping she didn't see her. She wasn't in the mood to talk.

Lina came around the corner. "I thought I saw you.

What are you doing?" She looked at the box in Carissa's hand. "Someone having snoring problems?"

Carissa straightened. "No, I was just looking for a friend."

"You know I heard of one anti-snoring remedy that costs nothing."

"What?" Carissa asked more curious than she wanted to be.

"Lose weight."

Oh how I hate you sometimes. "I see."

"It's true. It's scientifically proven. It's something your friend may want to think about."

"Hmmm."

"Or just get rid of the man who's complaining about it. I know Morris didn't try to make you change."

"I told you this is—"

"Come on, we're family and we both know this is for you. It's always a bad sign when a man makes you feel bad about yourself."

Carissa motioned her closer. "Okay, spill it. What do you have against Kenric?"

"I didn't say—" She stopped when Carissa fixed her with a hard stare. "I just don't think he's a good match for you. He doesn't fit in with us the way Morris did. Even your brother doesn't really like him, although he won't admit it. He usually gets on with just about everyone." She patted her stomach. "And the thought of a my little boy calling a man like Kenric 'Uncle' just sends shivers through me."

"You haven't said anything that makes sense. I'm

sorry you don't like him," Carissa said not meaning a word of it. "Because *I* do and that's not going to change."

She went to the cashier and bought the breathing strips feeling both annoyed and hurt. She didn't care what Lina thought of Kenric, but she was surprised that her brother had felt the same. She thought again about his strange response to meeting Kenric for the first time. What had that been about? Part of her wanted to ask him, but the other half didn't want to know the answer. Had she made another mistake that they saw and she didn't? She was a grown woman, she didn't need their approval and she wasn't going back to Morris just because they liked him better. But would their disapproval eventually drive Kenric away?

CHAPTER SEVENTEEN

"He's got her buying breathing strips," Lina told Glenn the moment he came through the front door after work.

"What?"

"Breathing strips. You know that thing to put over your nose to stop you from snoring," she said demonstrating the application. "That man she's seeing is forcing her to buy some."

"So what?"

"He's trying to change her. Morris never had her doing that."

"Lina," he said in a tired voice. "Leave it alone."

"I know you don't like him either, so stop defending him. Every time I mention his name you stiffen. You want to get rid of him as much as I do."

More, he wanted to say, but didn't. Riverton had rattled him, especially two days ago when he'd shown up at his office. He had been on lunch break, standing outside, enjoying one of the cigarettes he'd told his wife he'd stopped smoking when Riverton came up behind him.

"You didn't think I remembered you, did you?" he'd said.

Glenn didn't turn. He took a long drag on the cigarette, letting the sensation burn his lungs, trying to assess his next move. "My sister doesn't know."

"I thought as much."

He slowly spun around ready to face him. "She wouldn't believe you anyway, so there's no use mentioning anything."

"Really?"

"I've turned my life around. I was just doing what I had to do to get by."

"Supply and demand, right? It's not like you forced anyone to be your client, right?"

Glenn took another drag and grinned, glad he understood. "Yea."

"And when your little boy grows up, it won't be a big deal if someone makes him a client of their own?"

Glenn exhaled and watched the smoke float upward. "Are you threatening my family?"

"Just talking possibilities."

"They sound more like guesswork and I don't like guesses."

"And I don't like having to look at you right now," Riverton said in a grim tone. "But I'm stomaching it."

Glenn looked at him, although it was an effort, he didn't want to admit how much Riverton scared him. "What do you want? Want to try to finish me off? Imagine if I told my sister how violent you are."

"I don't plan to have any secrets between us."

"How about you and the rest of the world? Wouldn't it be awful for people at the office to find out the real relationship you are having with her?"

Riverton narrowed his gaze. "You'd hurt her that way?"

"You'd hurt her even more if you told her about me. I think we can both agree that we care about Carissa. You keep my secret and I'll keep yours."

But as he listened to his wife continue to complain about Riverton, he knew he'd offered an empty threat. He could keep him quiet for awhile, but not forever. Soon their private affair wouldn't need to be a secret. And what if Riverton used his sister to get revenge on him? But then again, Riverton hadn't known he was Carissa's brother until after he'd gotten involved with her. Maybe it was real. Maybe he really did care about Carissa. Glenn sniffed at the thought. That was wishful thinking. Riverton hated his guts. He knew he wouldn't stick around long. He felt sorry for his sister, but it would be for the best.

Besides, he hadn't done anything wrong. He'd held up his end of the deal, why bring up the past anyway? Through his sources, he knew that Riverton was worth even more now than he had been back then.

"Are you listening to me at all?" Lina asked.

"Yea, sure," he said flipping through the mail.

"We have to break them up. Ow!"

He glanced up alarmed. "What is it?"

"I stubbed my toe. Just the thought of him makes me so mad."

"Come on and sit down. You shouldn't upset yourself."

"You should have seen the way your sister spoke to me in the store. And those earrings she was wearing were so expensive."

"He's got money."

"And I'll bet you he'll become stingy with it."

He took her hand. "Don't worry, if I read him right, I don't think he'll be around for long."

Her eyes brightened and she smiled. "You really think so?"

He took her hand and kissed it; glad he could make her smile. "Yes, I do."

"I wish I could stay," Kenric said as he and Carissa stacked the dishwasher after dinner. "But I have to go away for a few days."

"Oh, great, I bought them for nothing," Carissa grumbled, thinking of her breathing strips.

"What?"

"Never mind."

"While I'm gone there's something I want you to consider."

"What is it?"

"Every year my parents host a party on the Potomac and I'd like to take you."

"You want me to meet your parents?"

He nodded.

"But—"

"Just think about it. The event isn't until several weeks so you don't have to make a decision now. I'll be leaving Simus Labs soon and then we can be open about our relationship and I thought that would be a good start."

"Okay," Carissa said trying not to sound as panicked as she felt. He wanted her to meet his parents?

He grinned then kissed her on the cheek. "Good."

She walked him to the door, missing him already. "Well, enjoy your trip."

"It'll be boring but that's business for you." He kissed her on the mouth and opened the door. "And don't worry, I saw what you bought. We'll be able to use those nose strips when I get back."

She slammed the door shut on the sound of his laughter.

CARISSA KEPT herself busy in his absence, which basically consisted of grocery shopping and cooking with Malcolm. Her phone rang one evening as she was cleaning out her stove. She saw Lina's number and ignored it. A text came soon after then the phone rang three more times before it stopped. Minutes later someone pounded on the door.

"Carissa I really need you this time. Please."

Carissa stood in front of her front door and stared at it determined to resist.

The pounding grew. "Please Carissa. I'm in labor."

She threw up her hands in surrender. She didn't

want her disturbing the neighbors. She swung open the door and saw Lina, a thin layer of sweat on her face, her cheeks red. She breathed a sigh of relief and rubbed the side of her stomach. "Why didn't you answer my call?" she demanded pushing past Carissa.

"I told you I wouldn't. Did you call Glenn?"

"You can call him at the hospital," Lina said taking a seat at the dining table. "You can get my suitcase and then drive me to the hospital."

"That wasn't the plan. You were supposed to call Glenn and then take a taxi."

"That was only if no one else was around. I don't want to take a taxi or anything else. I want you to drive me."

"No."

"What?"

"I'll get your suitcase, but that's it."

"Do you know how hard it is for a woman in labor to walk down two flights of stairs?"

"You're doing well so far."

"I'm really in labor. Do you think I'm faking it?" she said through clenched teeth.

"No, but if the contractions were really close together you wouldn't be sitting here so calmly."

She folded her arms. "I'm not leaving until you say yes."

"I can outlast you."

Lina laughed. "I doubt it."

Carissa's phone rang. She looked at the number and saw it was Kenric. "Hi."

"I wasn't going to call you today, but I couldn't stop myself."

Lina looked at her appalled. "Are you really going to talk to your boyfriend while I'm in labor!"

"What's going on?" Kenric asked concerned.

"Lina thinks she's in labor."

"I am in labor," she shouted.

Carissa shot her a glance. "Then call your husband."

"No."

"I should let you go," Kenric said.

Carissa sighed, disappointed that she wouldn't be able to talk to him more. "Sorry about this."

"It's okay, I could tell you stories about some of my brother's women."

"Carissa, I'm serious!" Lina said.

She squeezed her eyes shut. "An ambulance may be coming here for another reason, if I don't get rid of her soon."

He laughed. "Remember to breathe. Bye."

"Bye," she said then hung up.

Lina walked up to her and pointed. "I'm not going in an ambulance. I want you to get my suitcase and take me to the hospital now."

Carissa pushed her aside and turned on the TV.

Lina fell down beside her. "You can't treat me this way." She winced then swore. "We're family."

Carissa kept her gaze on the screen. She wouldn't be manipulated anymore. She wouldn't let her bully her. It stopped now.

After the first hour she heard some grunts and moans and groans but soon they quieted. When Carissa finally looked over at Lina she was fast asleep. She gripped her hands into fists. So much for labor pains. She felt like shaking her awake and shouting at her for continuing to play such a dangerous game. She didn't understand the need. Everyone adored her, wasn't that enough? Why did she always need to have Carissa come running?

After another hour Lina woke up, yawned and stretched her arms over her head.

"How are the labor pains?" Carissa asked in a flat tone.

Lina let her hands fall to her stomach and flashed a sheepish grin. "I guess it was a false alarm. I wasn't lying. I did feel them this morning and I was scared."

"I'm sure you were."

"I guess coming here calmed me." She yawned again. "I didn't realize I was so tired."

"Then you should go home and sleep."

"Couldn't you just make me a little something to eat?"

"No."

She pushed her lower lip out in a pout. "Please."

Before she could reply someone knocked on the door. When Carissa opened it she saw her brother. He looked past her and grinned at his wife. "I thought I'd find you here."

"And you can take her to go find something to eat," Carissa said.

"Couldn't she have something here?" he asked.

"No."

"Why not?"

"Because she's a little angry with me," Lina said. "It was a false alarm."

He rushed over to her, sat by her side and held her hand. "You were in labor?"

"I thought I was, so I came here and now Carissa thinks I made it up."

He turned to his sister. "You don't really think that, do you? How could you be angry with her? She didn't know it was a false alarm."

Carissa wasn't in the mood to argue. When it came to his wife everyone else was always the enemy. "I'm really not in the mood to prepare anything. If you want to eat you can get it yourself."

"Fine," Lina said starting to stand. She paused halfway, gasped and slowly sat back down, grabbing both sides of her stomach.

Glenn looked at her anxious. "What's wrong?"

"Something funny just happened." Her face brightened. "I think I really am in labor. That contraction was stronger than the rest."

"Are you scared?"

"No," she said with a note of awe. "We're soon going to hold our new baby boy in our hands. It's exciting."

He jumped to his feet. "Let me go get the suitcase. I'll be right back," he said and darted out the door.

Lina stood and stared at Carissa triumphant. "Isn't this amazing? In a few hours I'm going to be a mom and I'm not frightened at all. Now this is what I want you to do. You'll drive Glenn and me to the hospital. I want my husband in the backseat with me, holding my hand."

"I'm not going to the hospital with you. When Glenn returns he's taking you."

"What?"

"You heard me."

"But I want you to be there. I don't want to do this alone."

"You won't be alone. You'll have your husband and when you call her, your mother and then my mother too."

"But you *have* to be there. I'm really in labor this time."

"But you weren't last time?"

Her expression tightened. "I told you, it was a false alarm."

"I wish I could believe you, but I don't and that's the problem."

Lina folded her arms. "I'm not leaving until you say you'll take us."

"Suit yourself."

"I'm serious," Lina said resuming her seat on the couch.

"So am I."

"Okay, baby I'm back," Glenn said coming through the door.

"I'm not going," she said.

"What do you mean you're not going? Has the pain stopped?"

"Carissa said she won't come and I won't leave without her." She suddenly winced then groaned.

Glenn looked at his sister with panic. "Come on, Carissa. It's time."

"Then take her," she said. "I'm not coming."

He looked down at his wife. "Come on you don't want the contractions to get any worse."

Lina closed her eyes and let out a long breath. "I'll be fine as long as I'm not over stressed because of tension."

"You should go with your husband."

She glared at her. "I'm not going anywhere until you say 'yes'."

"You know your stubbornness could really put your life in danger," Carissa said.

"Just say you'll come," Glenn said.

"No," she turned and headed for the kitchen.

"Please, just do what she wants," her brother said. "Just this once."

"It's never 'just once.' It will be forever and I won't take it anymore. You and the rest of the family can spoil her but I won't. I don't think she'll last much longer when the real pain starts to hit and she stops smiling. Just wait another couple of minutes and she'll change her mind."

But Lina was more stubborn than Carissa thought and after another hour her breathing had become a little more shallow with mixtures of painful gasps and anguished groans that increased in depth and volume.

"It hurts so bad," Lina whimpered, grasping onto her husband like a pitiful child. "And she won't do anything."

He sent Carissa a glare, but the look she sent him quelled any rebuke. She had a stronger will than he did and he knew it. He returned his attention to his wife. "Lina, you're being ridiculous. Are you ready to go now?"

Lina bit down on her lip and let a contraction pass then said, "No." She shifted her glance to Carissa, the look of excitement and triumph gone from her face. "Why are you doing this to me?"

"I'm not doing anything. You're the one who's punishing yourself. By now you could be in a comfortable hospital bed with your husband by your side."

"I want you there."

"I'll be there later."

"I want you there *now*. I want you to drive us—"

"No."

Lina sat forward, resting her hands on her thighs, sitting in an inelegant pose. She hung her head and let out a deep breath.

Glenn reached for her. "Lina."

"Get me some water," she snapped.

"But—"

"Now!"

He hurried into the kitchen.

She looked at Carissa. "I liked you a lot more when you were with Morris. You weren't so selfish and uncaring. I don't know what's come over you, but since you got your new look you're not the same and I don't like it. You think because you now have a rich man and get a couple of expensive gifts that you're above us?"

"No."

"The Carissa I knew before wouldn't watch me in pain and do nothing about it."

"Let your husband take you to the hospital."

She pointed to herself. Her face was flush, her hair plastered to her forehead by sweat. "Do you see this? Do you see what I'm about to do? I'm about to bring new life into this world. And you refuse to be there to support me? You're not doing anything more important than this. You owe me."

Glenn came back holding a glass of water and handed it to his wife. She took a long swallow.

"I think you may have to carry her to the car if she keeps this up for another hour," Carissa said. "Although the contractions do seem to come in different time intervals, so there's space. And her water hasn't broken yet." She looked at Lina flashing a sour grin. "And my couch thanks you."

Lina glared at her. "Don't be a bitch."

Carissa shot her brother a look of disdain. "Are you really going to let her keep this up?"

"Carrie, please."

Carissa surged to her feet. "No, this is the last time I'm going to tell you about the husband you need to be because you're soon going to be a father and you need to exert yourself." She walked over to Lina. "Because you're a lot stronger than she is and she's not thinking rationally so you have to do that for her. You take her under her arm and yank her to her feet," she said demonstrating, surprising them both. "Then take her to the car and drive her to the hospital."

Lina yanked her arm away. "My man treats me like a princess. He treats me with kid gloves. You're the problem. Do you really want me to give birth in your living room?"

"No."

"Then why can't you do this one thing?"

"Because I'm sick of you. I'm sick of you taking me for granted. How dare you say that I owe you. You and my brother decided to have a child. That's your choice, not mine. My life is just as valuable. I am proud of it. It's not perfect, but I'm glad I broke up with Morris, and I'm glad I'm wearing new clothes that make me feel good about myself."

"Carissa all I want—" Lina bent forward, lowered her head and squeezed her eyes shut as another wave of pain hit. She then released a breath and screamed, "Why are you doing this to me? You're supposed to take care of me! You're the only one in the family who cares about everybody else more than herself. That's the Carissa we love. And it will be your fault if anything happens to me or my baby!"

"No, it will be your fault. It will be your fault if you have to tell your son you gave birth to him on his Aunt's living room floor because you were too stubborn. Because you always want to have things your way. It's time to grow up Lina. This is the time you stop thinking just about yourself and start thinking about others. You're soon going to be a mother and have someone fully dependant on you. You won't be the center of attention anymore." She turned and looked at her brother. "And it's your fault too. How can you just stand by and watch this without doing anything? Stop acting so helpless. Your son is in there, ready to come out. Will you be there to catch him? Or are you going to let your wife try to hold him in so that she can prove a point?"

Glenn grabbed his wife's arm in a grip that made no allowance for struggle. "We're leaving now."

"I'll make you pay for treating me this way," she said as her husband dragged her to the door. "It'll serve you right if anything happens to me or my baby. I'll never forgive you for this and I'll make damn sure that you never see your nephew," she said, and she would have walked out of the door in a cloud of victory if another contraction hadn't seized her causing her to lean heavily against her husband as her knees buckled under the pain.

Their eyes met over Lina's bent head and she saw her brother's pleading gaze. Carissa knew what he planned to do next and she would help him, because he knew her limit. Carissa grabbed the suitcase and opened the front door while he lifted Lina in his arms and carried her. She followed him to the elevators and pushed the down button. As they descended she saw Lina wrap her arms around Glenn's neck and rest her head against his shoulder. She caught a small satisfied grin. Lina had a right to be pleased with herself. Glenn was a wonderful man and truly loved her. Soon she'd have a son who'd love her just as much.

Her hateful, spiteful words still rang in Carissa's ears. Even if she hadn't meant them, even if it was just the pain talking, they had wounded her. *You owe me. What do you have better to do?* She spoke to her as if her life was less valuable. She envied their love. She couldn't imagine Kenric carrying her to their car. They were both too practical for such romantic gestures. She'd likely meet him at the hospital. He wouldn't bend over backwards to please her as Glenn did. Maybe Lina had a right to feel so entitled, woman used to being so loved likely felt superior.

Once they reached the main lobby she saw Kenric coming through the front doors. He looked at them surprised and held a door open.

"Did something happen?" He looked at Carissa, taking the suitcase from her. "I thought you'd be back from the hospital by now."

"It's a long story," she said.

He followed them to the car and placed the suitcase in the trunk while Glenn settled his wife inside the passenger seat.

"Talk to you later," Glenn said to Carissa then jumped into the driver's seat and drove off.

"Are you going to follow them in your car?" Kenric asked.

I'll make damn sure that you never see your nephew, Lina's words sliced her because she knew she probably meant them. She knew her sister-in-law could be vengeful enough to deny her one of her greatest joys. She'd hosted her baby shower, cooed over all her photos showing her expanding belly, helped her shop for baby items and thought of names and now she wouldn't be able to see her brother's son. She turned to Kenric, seeing the look of confusion on his face. "No," she said, then covered her face and cried.

CHAPTER EIGHTEEN

He wrapped his arms around her and held her tight.
"Let me guess. You and Lina had a fight."

"The worse we've ever had."

"Want me to take you away for a few days?"

She shook her head.

Kenric held Carissa in his arms, the brilliant rays of
the setting sun painting the sky above an array of
different pinks and blues, but all he saw was gray. He'd
never felt so helpless and it angered him. He hated not
knowing what to do. That he couldn't stop her tears. He
could buy a lot of things, but not what she wanted. He
wanted to protect her, shield her from the callousness of
others, but he knew that was impossible. He wanted to
take her away, to get her mind off things, but he knew
part of his desires were selfish. If she was estranged from
her brother that would make things easier for him. He
wanted York out of his life—their lives. But Carissa had

refused his offer to take her away and he'd run out of ideas.

"She's right," Carissa said in a choked voice.

"About what?"

"If anything happens to her or the baby they'll blame me. I'm just so tired of being used."

"I'm sure everything will be fine," he said, hating the sound of his own voice and how pathetic and empty his words were. He didn't know what the future held and knew he couldn't make promises.

She sniffed then paused, then sniffed again, leaning closer into his jacket. "What's that smell?" She sniffed again. "It smells like chocolate."

"It's nothing," he said drawing away.

But she didn't believe him. She opened his jacket, reached inside his inner pocket and pulled out a designer chocolate bar.

He'd remembered her telling him the story of how during the summer, she'd save most of her babysitting money to contribute to her family's household expenses, but her one treat she didn't spare was buying herself a gourmet chocolate bar. It was one of her few luxuries. He'd hoped to treat her with one.

She stared down at the bar, running her fingers over the elaborate logo, then sniffed it. "Is this for me?"

"Yes. I thought it would be a fun way to celebrate becoming an Aunt."

Carissa wiped her eyes. "It's just what I need." She unwrapped the bar then broke a piece off and ate it. She squeezed her eyes shut. "Oh, it's as good as I remembered." She opened her eyes then broke off a piece and handed it to him. "Try it."

Kenric shook his head. "Watching you enjoy it is good enough for me."

"Fine," she said popping another piece in her mouth. "I won't force you,"

The chocolate had been an inspired idea, but he was glad it had stopped her tears, at least for a little while. "Do you want to go inside?"

She shook her head.

"Want to sit in the car?"

She shook her head again, then looked up at the sky. "I just want to stand right here and finish this while the sun sets."

"Okay."

She ate a few more bites then took one piece, rubbed it against her lips, then she kissed him. "That was my special chocolate kiss. Did you like it?"

He licked his lips. "I thought it was delicious."

"Would you like another one?"

"Yes, but only when we're inside. Are you ready?"

She looked up at the building and took a deep breath. "I'm afraid of what I'll remember. I'm afraid of thoughts running over and over in my mind and the words she said."

"You don't have to be afraid. I'm here with you and if you give me another chocolate kiss, I'll make sure that the only thing you're thinking about is me."

"That's a big promise."

He smiled. "I like to deliver on my promises." And moments later he did.

"Why aren't you here?"

Carissa knew the call would come, so she'd been prepared for it. However, she'd expected the pleading tone of her mother, instead of her father's demanding voice. "Is Lina okay?"

"If you were here you'd know."

"Glenn's there. You can depend on him. Despite what you think, he's a good man."

She heard something shatter in the background. She hurried to the kitchen and saw Kenric picking up pieces of broken glass.

"Use a broom or you'll cut yourself," she said, pointing to the closet.

"Sorry," he said.

"Who's there with you?" her father asked.

"None of your business."

"Are you there with a man? Are you that shameless? You'd prefer to be with some man rather than at your sister-in-law's side?"

"Yes, Dad. So what name are you going to call me that I haven't heard before?"

He fell silent.

"How many pounds?" she couldn't help asking.

"He hasn't come yet. There were complications."

"What kind of complications?"

"Women's stuff. How the hell would I know?"

"Is mom there? Put her on the phone."

"If you really want to know what's going on, get your ass over here."

He disconnected.

She swore. She wouldn't put it past Lina to get sick just to spite her. She wanted her at the hospital one way or another. "I'm not going," she said aloud. "There's nothing I can do anyway."

Kenric came into the room. "What's going on?"

"My father said there's been a complication, but he won't tell me what. He's as bad as she is." She dialed her mother's cell phone but she wouldn't answer. She left a message for her brother, not expecting a reply. She paced then screamed in frustration. "I don't want to care, but I do!"

"I'm sure if something was really bad, your mother would have called you." He pulled her close and held her.

"You're right. My father wants me to feel guilty for having my own life." She took a deep breath. "Lina's fine. The baby's fine. Everything will be fine."

An hour later she discovered she was right when her brother sent her a simple text: 9LBS. 8 OUNCES.

CHAPTER NINETEEN

IT WAS DONE. Over. Three months had flown by so fast. The slight chill of autumn was already starting to touch the leaves. Change was in the air. Carissa looked at Kenric as he held his final meeting with the department heads. The deal with Barra Industries was done and all the transitions had been made. His job was done and he was leaving. She couldn't believe they'd managed to keep their affair secret this long and although he promised to continue their relationship, visiting her on weekends, she knew that things would never be what it was.

The henchman was going. Her first thought of him still made her smile. She'd never have envisioned what an essential part he'd be in her life. Not just as a lover, but also as a friend. He no longer joked about becoming husband number three and she missed that, but she knew that wasn't logical. Their lives were too different and although she knew that's what she wanted, she wouldn't pressure him. She'd pressured Morris and had lost him, she didn't want to do the same with Kenric.

The sound of applause woke her out of her thoughts. She joined in and plastered on a smile. As much as she'd prepared for this moment, she didn't want him to go. She left the conference room and walked to the elevator in a bit of a daze. The conversation of others buzzing around her.

"Glad to see him go," one said.

"Surprised we were still left in one piece," another chimed in.

"Ms. York?"

Carissa spun around when Kenric called her name. In all the months at Simus Labs, he'd never called her out, specifically not in front of others. She approached him with caution. "Yes, Mr. Riverton?"

In one forward motion, she was in his arms and his mouth covered hers. Before she could respond to his passionate embrace, he released her. His face spread into a satisfied smile. "I had to get that out of my system." He nodded to the shocked crowd then left.

Carissa raced to the stairs, not knowing exactly how to feel or respond, the voices of her colleagues drifting towards her.

"They were really having an affair?" one said.

"I knew it all along," another chimed in.

"When did this happen?" a third asked.

"I bet it's a prank," a fourth added. "Where are the cameras?"

Carissa ran down the stairs then darted into her office and closed the door. She took a deep breath then pulled out her phone and called him. "What were you thinking?!"

"I wanted to leave in style," Kenric said without a note of remorse.

"You're going to have the rumor mill going for months."

"It won't be a rumor anymore. It's the truth."

"Kenric—"

"I'm sorry, you looked so beautiful today I couldn't help myself."

She sighed. It was hard to be angry with him after a line like that. "You're—"

"The man who's in love with you, so treat me to lunch. I'll meet you in the lobby at twelve-fifteen," he said, then hung up.

In love with her? Did he really say he was in love with her? First he was kissing her in public and now this? Was this some sort of strange goodbye? His life wasn't here. Did he expect her to move to be with him? Carissa was in the lobby at twelve-ten. She noticed the looks from other employees, but for once, didn't care. Then she heard a squeal and inwardly groaned. She hadn't thought about Ashley.

"Oh my God?" Ashley said. "Is it true? You're with Riverton?"

"Yes."

She squealed again.

Carissa delicately touched her ears. "Stop doing that."

"You've got to give me the details. How did you do it? He's scary as hell."

"He's not scary."

"Maybe not to you." She grinned. "You found his soft side huh? You sly dog." She nudged her with her elbow. "Let me take you to lunch."

"I already have an appointment."

"With him? Oh yes, I see him coming this way. I'll dash, but fill me in later." She hurried off.

Carissa turned to Kenric. "I—" She started to say, but he kissed her instead.

"Stop that."

"I can't help myself. You don't know how many times I dreamed of doing that in the conference room. Now everybody knows you're mine."

Carissa couldn't help a smile. "Barra Industries next takeover?"

He shook his head. "No, this is purely Riverton interest." He took her hand and walked to the front entrance of the building. "Let's eat."

After lunch they walked along the main road then he stopped in front of a shop and looked at the display window.

"What do you see?" he asked.

"I see a store. Why? What do you see?"

"I see the reflection of a man standing next to the woman he wants to marry."

Carissa turned to him stunned. "You're not serious."

"Do you think I'm the type of man to joke about these things?"

"But—"

His eyes clung to hers. "You don't want to marry me?"

"No, that's not it."

An easy smile played at the corners of his mouth. "Then we'll work out the rest. You've made me happier than you'll ever know."

"Kenric—"

"My parent's party is in two weeks. We'll keep our engagement between us for now. We'll look at rings next week."

"This is all happening so fast. Where will we live? What about your job? My job?"

"My job is a lot more flexible than yours and there are a number of options I've been considering. Also, I think I have an idea of where we could live that I want to show you."

The next day Carissa found herself standing inside a house that left her breathless. She barely noticed the coffered ceiling, the French doors leading to a balcony or the six bedrooms. No, all she saw were the windows. Dozens of floor-to-ceiling picture windows that allowed light to flood in from all directions. She'd never lived in a house before and never thought her first one would offer her such a luxury.

"What do you think?" Kenric asked as they stood in the gourmet kitchen after touring the house. The real estate agent had discreetly left them alone.

Carissa stared at him, not knowing what to say. "I love it, but..." She glanced around the spacious kitchen and the adjacent breakfast room.

"But what?"

She hesitated, not wanting to disappoint him. She saw that he'd casually rested his hand on the countertop, but it was balled in a fist. She could see his knuckles were pale and she sensed how much he wanted to please her. She covered his hand with hers. "I do love it, but there's just one thing that bothers me."

"What?"

"How will we clean all the windows?"

She felt his fist relax under her hand and his face softened into a smile. "Darling, we'll hire people for that. You won't have to clean anything."

"Oh," Carissa said feeling a little foolish for her naiveté. She pushed away the feeling and hugged him. "Then it's perfect."

"Great," he said wrapping his arms around her. "I'll make the arrangement." He drew away, keeping his arms around her waist, and looked down at her. "However, there are certain things I have to take care of first."

"That sounds a bit ominous."

She expected him to smile, but instead his expression grew serious. "Promise me that no matter what happens you'll stay by my side and trust me."

"Trust you? Why wouldn't I trust you?"

He shrugged. "Life is full of surprises," he said, but although his tone was light, his words left her with a heavy feeling.

"You wouldn't believe what I saw your brother doing," Jackie said coming out of the bathroom after finishing her shower.

Joshua lay on his bed and watched her pour lotion on

her hand then lather her legs. "What?" he asked with little interest. He knew Kenric was back in town, but hadn't spoken to him since that night they'd argued and knew it would be awhile before he could face him again.

"Looking at rings."

He sat up. "What?"

"Yea, I know, isn't it crazy? I was in the store. You know that jeweler—"

Joshua watched her mouth move, not caring where the jeweler was, wishing she'd get to the point.

"—and I overheard him saying he was bringing in his fiancée next week or something."

Joshua gripped the bed sheets into his fists. He was marrying that bitch? Despite all they knew? Despite what he said? Was Kenric really that blind? Maybe Jackie got it wrong. She misunderstood. Kenric wouldn't take a risk like that.

But three hours later, Joshua received a phone call that confirmed it.

"You would not believe it," his mother said over the phone. "Your brother just asked for an extra table setting for his girlfriend. *Girlfriend.* He never brings anyone. He's as much told us that he's ready to settle down. Unlike some," she said in a pointed voice, Joshua chose to ignore. "Do you know who she is?"

He gritted his teeth. His brother was taking it too far, but Joshua didn't want to upset his mother with the truth. "Not really."

"Annoying boy. He can be such a dark horse. He wouldn't even tell me her last name. Just said her name was Ressa."

"Carissa."

"Yes, that's it! Are you sure you're not hiding something?"

"No. Sorry Mom, I've got to go."

"Always on the run. I won't bother you. I'll see you at the party. But please bring someone who speaks English this time." She hung up.

No, Kenric was not introducing Carissa to his parents. He was not going to let his brother make that woman part of his family. Since his brother wasn't going to listen to him, he was going to have to try another tactic. He picked up the phone and dialed.

CARISSA LOOKED around the park wondering why Kenric's brother wanted to meet her there. She knew he lived out of state, so found it odd that he wanted to talk to her in person. When she saw him, she smiled and waved. He didn't smile back.

"I'll make this quick," he said walking up to her. "How much do you want?"

She blinked surprised by the anger in his tone. "What?"

"There's no use playing games, I know how your family works. Just give me a figure."

"I don't know what you're talking about."

He pointed at her and flashed a triumphant grin. "Yes, that's what I came down here to see. That innocent look. You're good. Attractive enough, smart, but I still wanted to see how you've been able to wrap my brother around your finger. I see it now, but it won't work with me. I know women and I know most have a hidden agenda, which is why I don't tie myself down to one. You must already be planning the wedding. How much will it cost to cancel it and let my brother free?"

"I love your brother—"

"Really? You love him so much that you're prepared to ruin his life? Most of the people will be hiding their laughter the moment they see you in a white dress walking down the aisle."

Carissa winced, surprised by the cruelty of his words. She couldn't understand why he was so angry. "He already knows I've been married before and I have no intention of wearing white."

"Ahh...so you *do* plan to marry him."

She didn't want to get caught, since Kenric wanted their engagement kept a secret for a while. "We've talked about it, but nothing's official yet."

"You shouldn't even be talking about something you don't deserve."

"I don't need to hear this."

She started to walk past him, he grabbed her arm. "You say you love my brother, but did you see his face when he had to bury our sister because of what your brother did?"

Carissa stared at him, not sure she'd heard him correctly. "My brother? What are you talking about?"

"You're still going to pretend that you don't know?" Joshua paused, then studied her face. "Or maybe you really don't know. He was good. Perhaps he fooled you too. He certainly fooled us."

"My brother is a good man and he's never hurt anyone."

"Of course, I'd expect that kind of loyalty from you. I'm loyal too. Admittedly to only a few things, but they mean a lot to me and one of them is my family. Most of all, my brother. You have no idea what he's gone through. No idea how the sight of his tears at our sister's gravesite are etched in my memory. In your eyes, your brother is probably a saint, so you won't believe a word I have to say."

"What did my brother do?" she asked afraid to move.

He seemed surprised by the question and for a long moment just stared at her, as if he didn't know what to do. "Ask Kenric," he finally said. "And watch his face. If you truly love him, you'll call me with a price and get out of our lives."

CHAPTER TWENTY

Kenric walked up to Carissa's apartment whistling. He hadn't felt this good in years. No merger, takeover or negotiation coup had ever made him feel this alive and triumphant. He'd convinced Carissa to share her life with him and he knew it would be one fun ride. He'd never loved Fridays as much as today. All week, he'd been looking forward to spending the weekend with Carissa and now he could. He stopped when he saw Malcolm sitting on the stairwell landing looking glum.

"What's up? Had a bad day at school?"

Malcolm shook his head. "Miss Carissa came back looking upset. We were supposed to pick up some groceries to make brownies, but she cancelled."

Kenric swore. Had Lina upset her again? He patted the boy on the shoulder. "Thanks for the warning. Don't worry, I'll make sure she doesn't make her double fudge brownies without you."

He hurried up the rest of the stairs and knocked.

When Carissa opened the door he knew something was seriously wrong.

"What did my brother do to your sister?" she asked.

He should have been expecting the question. He had been preparing for it, knowing he wouldn't be able to keep it a secret from her forever, but the moment happened sooner than he'd hoped.

He stepped inside and closed the door. "What do you know?"

"I don't know anything, I just had a strange conversation with your brother in the park."

Kenric paused. "He came down here to see you?"

"Yes."

He was going to get Joshua back for that. "Sit down," Kenric said, searching his mind for the best way to handle the situation.

"No, just tell me what happened."

Kenric shoved his hands in his pockets. "It was a long time ago."

"Did he assault her?"

"No. It happened nearly fifteen years ago and I spoke to him—"

Her eyes flashed. "You spoke to him and you didn't tell me?"

He swore, that had been a wrong move. "I didn't want you to know yet."

"Why not?"

"Because of this. Because I knew you'd be angry at me for what I did."

"What did you do? What did my brother do? How

could you both have kept this from me? I don't even know what *this* is!"

"Carissa, I know you must be curious, but let's just focus on us right now."

She headed to the door. "If you won't tell me then I'll get my brother to."

He grabbed her arm. "Okay, wait, wait," he said in surrender. "I'll tell you. But please, I need you to sit down."

She did and waited.

He took a deep breath; the action seeming to hurt as the memories came flooding back. Why had his brother brought it up? Why couldn't he have waited? He had a plan and it could have worked.

"Kenric," Carissa said when he remained silent.

He gazed down at her. "Do you remember your promise?"

"My promise?"

"That you'd stay by my side and trust me?"

Carissa shook her head, her eyes filling with tears. "Right now I don't trust anyone. First I have your brother saying awful things to me and implying that my brother did something terrible. Then I discover that you spoke to him behind my back and that he's keeping something from me too. Don't you *dare* ask me to trust you when you've lied to me by omission."

He nodded. "You're right, but I thought I was protecting you."

"From what? From you or from him?"

Carissa regretted the words the moment she said them.

She'd wanted to spur him on to speak but had hurt him, instead, she saw a look of devastation crossing his face and then she remembered Joshua's words about the sight of his tears at his sister's gravesite. She had her anger, but she had to consider his pain and consider that his actions—though wrong, had been for her benefit. "I'm sorry," she said taking his hand, and tugging him to sit down beside her. "I didn't mean that. I'd never be afraid of you. I'm just...I feel betrayed and your brother looked as if he hated me."

Kenric's gaze hardened to granite. "He shouldn't have done that. You're innocent and this has nothing to do with you."

She held his hand in both of hers then brought it to her mouth and kissed it. "I'm strong enough to hear whatever you have to say. Please tell me."

He took a deep breath, but something about her action seemed to relax him. He realized that he also needed her trust. That no matter what he said that she'd listen to him, even if she didn't believe him. "We had a vacation home down here fifteen years ago where we all used to come. I had a sister who was..." He shook his head. "I don't know the best word for it really. Lost, I guess. She had everything money could buy except happiness, although we all tried our best to give it to her. Unfortunately, she found it on her own one day—first in a nice sweet smoke then an ugly little pill and finally in a beautiful white powder. I was able to keep most of her suppliers away, except for one. He was newer, young, about eighteen at the time, and ambitious and more dangerous. Twice he'd 'loaned' my sister out for favors. The drugs were bad enough, but I wasn't going to let him turn her into a prostitute as well, so I thought I could make him a deal. I had the arrogance of the twenty-two year old I was at the time, that I could handle anything with money. I gave him nearly sixty thousand dollars to stay away from my sister. He agreed, took the money and disappeared from our lives. Within a year my sister was clean and on her way to a better life.

"Then the following summer I came down to the family vacation home for a visit and opened the door to the sound of my younger brother's screams. I found my sister unresponsive on the bedroom floor. I called the ambulance then I looked up and saw a reflection in the mirror someone was in the closet. I pulled him out and when I recognized him, I grabbed a hanger and nearly killed him. He escaped when the EMTs arrived, but it was too late for my sister. He had taken my money and lied to me. He watched my sister take her last fatal dose. I never thought I'd see him again until the night I had dinner with your brother."

Carissa let Kenric's hand go. "You must have him confused with someone else. My brother had entered college on a full scholarship at the time."

"What was the name of the scholarship? Did you see the application? Was it—"

"No, but you can't be sure."

Kenric smiled without humor. "You think I'd forget the face of the man I tried to kill?"

Carissa shook her head. It was too unimaginable to believe. Her brother didn't deal drugs—and prostitution? That was ludicrous! He was as clean as they came. He was driven, the smart one. The one who had made their family proud.

"I know it's hard to wrap your mind around, but it was him. With my money he paid for his education, his food and his shelter and his chance for a better life while he preyed on my sister and others like her."

Carissa's mind spun in bewilderment. He wasn't talking about Glenn. It wasn't possible. "But why would he? We weren't raised—"

"He remembered me Carissa. Why do you think that is?"

She shook her head, unable to face him. She stared blindly out the window. "I don't know."

"I let him know that I remembered him."

"And what did he say?" she asked in a hollow voice, feeling empty.

"He didn't deny that we'd met before, but said he didn't supply her last dose."

"And did you believe that?"

"No, but I can't change it. Nothing will bring my sister back. But I don't want to think about the past. I want—"

"You should go."

"I know you don't want to believe me—"

She stared at him. "That's the awful part. I do. So many things didn't make sense back then. His scholarship. His story about getting mugged. Kenric, I believe you." She pounded her chest with her fist, tears springing to her eyes. "And it's killing me."

He reached for her. "Carissa—"

She recoiled from his touch. "How can you even look at me?"

"What?"

"How can you even think of building a future with me?"

"We both know how we feel and we can work through this together," he said in a soft voice, his eyes pleading.

"How about your family? Will they accept me?"

"They will in time."

She wiped away her tears and shook her head. "You didn't see your brother's face."

"I will handle my brother."

"And at your parent's fancy party do you want me to pretend that I don't have two exes, that I lack a college degree and that my brother was the dealer who may have been responsible for your sister's death?"

"No, you don't have to pretend to be anything, and I'll make sure none of that comes up."

"I can't marry you Kenric." She stood. "You should go. No, I won't marry you."

He stood too. "Carissa."

"Not until I find out the truth."

"The truth doesn't matter."

"It matters to me. Right now, I can hardly look at you, how can I face your family?"

"You know he'll deny everything."

"He can deny all he wants. I'm used to dealing with liars," she said in a sour tone.

Kenric fell silent then ran a tired hand down his face.

"So you'll marry me after we find out the truth? Okay, then I'll—"

"No, not 'we'. Me," Carissa said tapping her chest, surprised that he could still talk about marrying her. "My family has hurt you enough. I have to uncover this on my own. Do you know why I believe you about Glenn? Because my family is filled with losers, liars and thieves. I thought he'd changed that and I thought I'd escaped it, but I didn't. Having you by my side would be like throwing a beautiful golden ball into the gutter."

"Are you sure you're not trying to protect your brother from me? Did he maybe hint at something about me?"

"He didn't tell me anything. I told you that. I believe your story."

"Then why are you pushing me away?"

"Because I need to find out more. On my own. Now please go."

He cradled her hand in his. "Promise you'll come back to me. I'll give you space and I'll give you time, just promise. I love you."

She kissed him, knowing that he wanted her to say that she loved him too, but her heart felt too broken to let her.

CHAPTER TWENTY-ONE

HE KNEW judgment day would come. Glenn saw the look on his sister's face and wordlessly gave his baby son to his wife before following her into the hall of the apartment. He had to play it cool, he'd let her reveal what she knew. He may be jumping to conclusions. Kenric didn't want to hurt her. He followed her to the courtyard, making sure to keep his expression casual although he felt tense.

"What was the name of the scholarship you won again?" Carissa asked.

"Why are you bringing that up?"

"Because I just figured out that Notrevir is Riverton spelled backwards, I thought that was an odd coincidence."

"Yes."

"But it's not. You took their money and lied to us."

"That was nearly—"

She slapped him. "You bastard. All this time looking

down on James when you followed in his footsteps. You just didn't get caught."

"I did what I had to do. Those people in their big houses in Washington DC lie to us all the time. They tell us to take minimum wage jobs that they've never held, to work our way up in companies when they use connections and money to get whatever they want. I knew I didn't have a chance to break the cycle. I didn't have any connections, but I realized I could make money. Besides, if I didn't sell it, someone else would. You wouldn't believe how much snow was falling in those rich neighborhoods and on those gleaming college campuses. I didn't owe them anything."

"You killed her."

"I didn't kill anyone. I shouldn't have been there I know, but an associate left something of mine at her place and I went to get it. She was already halfway through a bad batch when I saw her. I tried to do something, then I heard footsteps and hid. I really was out of the game by then, I swear. I was going to school for real. I graduated, remember? I didn't give her that last dose."

"And you think that makes everything alright?"

He couldn't help a nervous smile. Facing Riverton had been hard, but his sister's good opinion meant the world and her look of disgust was like a slow death. "I learned a lot about business," he said feigning disinterest.

"You think this is funny?"

"Look, it's over now."

"You lied to me. You lied to all of us."

"Do you really think there are keys to the castle? You couldn't afford college and you pressured me to go."

"Don't put this on me."

"I had no connections, no way to qualify for loans, my grades weren't going to get me far, what was I supposed to do?"

"Be a man, instead of a damn dog like the rest of the men in our family," she said then turned.

"We can't play by their rules, Carey," he called after her. "The odds are stacked against us for a reason. You'll never be part of their world and they'll never understand ours. A man like Kenric is out of your reach."

She spun around and glared at him with a rage he'd only seen in his father, who'd terrified him as a boy. "And you made certain of that."

SHE SMELLED BISCUITS. Carissa walked into her apartment and swore. Biscuits only meant one thing...

"You've been a bad girl," Sara said, closing the oven.

Carissa flopped down into her couch. "I don't need this right now."

"You're lucky I intervened. You haven't worn your third pair of stockings yet."

"Who cares about stockings? I—"

Sara set a plate of biscuits on the table. "Haven't looked at your instructions for weeks and I bet you haven't said your oath in while."

"I really don't--"

She sat in front of her. "I was instructed to come back before you ruined everything. They were going to send Rania." She sent Carissa a pointed look. "But that would have been ugly. She is not pleased with you, because you're ruining a good thing."

Carissa rubbed her forehead. *Who was Rania?* "I really don't care."

"In case you haven't noticed, you've gotten what we promised. Kenric loves you and he's not ashamed of you."

Carissa shook her head, fighting back tears. "It doesn't matter. I don't deserve to be his wife. I don't deserve to meet his family."

"You're not your brother."

"I'm ashamed that it took two failed marriages to finally find the right one, that—"

Sara held up her hand. "Excuse me, but have you missed the big point? He loves you."

"And I cannot accept that."

"Why not?"

"Because it's too precious a gift for someone like me."

"Remember the oath?"

"I don't give a damn about the stupid oath. All this shouldn't have happened to me. You should have chosen someone else. I'll never forget the look of pain on his face as he told me about his sister. He comes from a good family. To tie himself to us would be laughable and cruel."

"Are you worried about what other people will think again?"

"No, this is what *I* think."

Sara pulled out her cell phone then held up a picture of Carissa and Kenric laughing at the beach. "Why doesn't this man deserve this woman?"

"I didn't say he didn't deserve me, I said I didn't deserve him."

"I know what you said, but that's not my question. This woman here makes this man happy, he wants to spend his life with her. Does that make him stupid?"

"No."

"I'm here to support you because the next step will be hard."

"Next step?"

"Your third set of instructions are to wear your last pair of stockings to a place that scares you. Are you ready for that?"

She could already feel her palms getting sweaty. She knew what finding out the truth really entailed and she felt strangely bereft without Kenric. She'd learned to depend on him so much. "Yes, I'm ready. But do I really have to wear them there? Couldn't I—"

"No, you have to face your past."

CHAPTER TWENTY-TWO

Her past was a smooth looking man with golden-brown eyes and a slick grin. Her ex husband, James Pinker, could charm a bird out of the sky. It was his charm that had blinded her, he was also an expert liar. Although she'd told Kenric she was used to liars, James still scared her. This was his second time inside, but he'd be out soon and right back to doing what he'd always done. But she was determined to get the answers she needed, no matter the consequences.

"Baby girl you're looking fine," he said taking a seat in front of her and acting as if they were meeting in a fancy restaurant instead of the jail's visiting room. "Wow, how come you never dressed up like this for me before?"

Carissa glanced over at the bars on the windows, the sight a reminder of the cramped apartment she'd shared with him. "I have something to ask you."

"I'm doing well."

She shook her head. "That's wasn't it. Did you know about my brother?"

"Did I know what about your brother?"

"Don't play innocent with me, he told me you introduced him to your line of work."

He lifted his brows. "You got him talking? I'm surprised. Disappointed, really."

"So it's true?"

"I thought I was being generous, sharing my expertise with a younger man who wanted to improve himself." James grinned. "He was a natural."

"He was so good he killed a girl."

James yawned. "Your brother never killed anyone. If he said he did, he's just bragging."

"Bragging?"

"You know, trying to make himself look big."

"I know what it means, but how could anyone brag about killing someone?"

He looked at her as if she were naïve. "You know the world better than that, baby. Fear gets respect." He looked her up and down. And she knew he noticed her fitted two-piece outfit and chocolate colored fishnet stockings. "You know, they allow for conjugal visits."

"I'm seeing someone."

"He doesn't have to know."

Carissa ignored him. "Did you know anything about the Riverton overdose? It was about fifteen years ago. I know you used to keep track of them like it was a game."

"Not a game baby, business. I needed to know where my money was coming from. If a client died, I needed to get a new one."

"So what can you tell me about it?"

"Wasn't my route."

"James, you know something."

He scratched his cheek, thoughtful. "When your brother stopped supplying her she went to Cracker. You know like after...what was that...yea, Cracker Jacks? Do they still have those boxes with the little prize inside? He was the same. You were always in for a surprise. The worse kind out there. I always provided the highest quality. You could count on it, but his product was complete sh—"

"I get the point. Where is he?"

His expression grew serious. "Why do you want to know?"

"Because I have some questions."

"What are you doing? You found out about me and left this life years ago, why dreg it all up? Stay away baby, don't let your brother drag you down. You're a classy lady."

She sniffed. "No, I'm not, but you always were a good liar."

"It's the truth. Baby, I used to deliver to multi-million dollar mansions, Rolls and Bentleys, there was one chick who dropped twenty-five thou' a week on clothes, don't ask me how I know, I just like knowing the ones who can pay me. I saw them all, and sure they had money and degrees, but I could tell the classy ones from the money hoes. You know, the ones if you stripped them of their cash, they'd have nothing left. You may not have their shine, but you have the class."

"That's a really nice speech," Carissa said, sounding bored. "But it doesn't help me."

"I'll telling you to let this go. Your brother didn't kill anyone."

"I just need to verify—"

"Why? What does it have to do with you? So some rich girl died because she had nothing better to do, it happens all the time."

"I know her brother."

"So why isn't he here talking to me?" James glanced at her handbag. "You've got his balls in your purse or something?"

"I told him not to come."

"So he's letting you go after crap like Cracker to get the answers for him?"

"No, I told him—"

James' eyes widened. "And he listened to you? There's no way a real man would let his woman...." He paused then started to grin. "You didn't tell him what you were going to do, did you?" He winked. "I guess I did have a little influence over you? What does he think you're up to?"

"Just tell me where Cracker is or I'll find him myself." She stood, her plastic chair scraping along the concrete floor.

"You said he's one of the Rivertons?" He gave a low whistle. "You do aim your sights high. Let me guess, he's the mean one." He laughed at her expression. "Do you think information stops flowing because I'm in here?"

"All I want is a name."

"I want to meet him."

"That's not going to happen. If you won't help me, I'll find him myself."

"You think it'll be that easy? You think you can just do a search online?" he said miming typing on a keyboard. "That name's too common." He tapped the table. "If he's not man enough to come here, he doesn't deserve the truth."

She didn't want Kenric there. She didn't want him to meet James. But she knew he knew the major players and that could help Kenric. However, letting James know he was the one in control was always a bad move. She needed a different strategy.

He flashed a nasty grin. "And keeping secrets makes you no better than me."

What he said hurt her. He was right. She was doing to Kenric what James had done to her. Charming him with lies, manipulating him with tears. Didn't he deserve to know the truth too, no matter what the consequences? She should leave. She didn't want to be there. She glanced down at her stockings and then remembered the last part of the Black Stockings Society oath. *I will never settle for less.*

No, she wouldn't settle for James winning again, for her brother making her feel that Kenric was out of reach, or feel that she'd never leave her past behind. She looked at James with new eyes. He looked too cocky and assured of himself. She wasn't going to expose Kenric to him. James was her problem and she'd take care of him. She saw him clearly and knew who she was dealing with. He hated anyone who did well and she knew it was only a power move to have Kenric come to him. To have him on his territory. She wouldn't allow him that victory. Fortunately she knew he had weak spot.

"Heard your son's doing well," she said.

The cocky light in his eyes dimmed. "No need to mention him."

"Be a shame if he got caught with anything illegal."

"You leave my son—"

"Give me a name and address."

"I'm just trying to protect you."

"You never tried to protect anyone unless you got a payout. Now give me a name."

"It doesn't matter. He doesn't use that name anymore," James said, then told her what she wanted.

Carissa drove away from the jail, her hands shaking as she gripped the steering wheel. She'd survived and felt vindicated. James wanted to tear her down, but instead, she felt free. She knew the truth and she wouldn't be ashamed of her past anymore or her brother's. She looked at herself in the mirror and didn't mind what she saw. Now she could face the Rivertons. She couldn't before, when she had so many questions and she questioned her worth. It wasn't until this moment that she realized how much she'd hated being herself. How long she'd wanted to get away from her name. She'd married young so she could distance herself from it. Yorks weren't any good. Seeing her brother succeed had given her some pride back. Then to hear the truth ripped it away. Before, she couldn't feel Kenric's love for her, no matter how many times he said it. But now she could.

Because she was no longer ashamed of *who* she was and where she came from. Her brother's choices weren't hers. She had been able to face James, but knew there was one more person.

IT WAS SO UNFAIR, Lina thought as she slammed her car trunk closed and carried three bags of groceries towards the apartment's entrance. She saw a man ahead of her go inside the apartment complex and close the door behind him. She silently called him a foul name. When she was pregnant it was so much better, people were a lot more considerate. She struggled to open the door then headed to the elevators, seething and feeling sweaty. Even though the calendar said autumn the day still felt like summer. Right now she wished she could be at the pool.

She wouldn't even have to do this if Carissa hadn't changed. Carissa was supposed to be helping her with her duties as a new mother. She couldn't believe nobody wanted to help her. Her mother had lasted a week, her mother-in-law two. Was it her fault that Jeremy was a miserable baby? That he cried the moment he woke up and hardly stopped until he was asleep? Was it her fault that her nerves were always on edge? Even Glenn hadn't been his carefree self. If Carissa hadn't been so selfish none of this would have happened. She'd made the right decision to keep her out of their lives.

It wasn't fair, she fought back tears as she unpacked

her bags in the kitchen. She missed Carissa. She missed how much she took care of her. Why had she abandoned her at her greatest time of need? It was Kenric's fault. Kenric had changed her.

Glenn came into the kitchen as she put the final item away. "Do you need help?"

Lina looked at him annoyed and closed a cupboard. "I wish you'd asked me that five minutes ago."

He kissed her on the cheek. "I'm sorry." He looked around the kitchen. "Where's Jeremy? Is he taking a nap?"

Stark terror descended as a horrible realization struck her. Lina grabbed her keys and raced to the door.

"Where are you going?" Glenn called after her.

But she couldn't voice her shame—she'd left her baby in the car.

CHAPTER TWENTY-THREE

SCREAMS. He'd hoped never to hear screams like that again in his life, but he did—piercing, heartbreaking screams from somewhere in the parking lot. He'd planned to stay away from Carissa, but after a week, he couldn't. He'd come to her apartment to talk to her. As he got out of his car he heard the screams. Kenric scanned the area trying to assess the source and the danger.

Then he saw Lina holding a limp baby in her arms; Glenn running up behind her.

He ran over to them. "What happened?"

Lina continued to scream and Glenn stood looking helpless. "She left him in the car."

Kenric could tell he was in shock and she was hysterical. He knew he had to take the lead. "Call 911," he told Glenn then addressed Lina. "Give the baby to me."

"He's dead!" she cried out.

"He's not dead, he's suffered heatstroke but we can save him. Give him to me!" When she hesitated, he snatched the infant from her, knowing the risk he was taking if anything went wrong, but not caring. He darted inside and called out to the concierge at the front desk. "Where's your break room? I need to get the baby cooled down."

The guard led them to a back room where Kenric stripped the baby out of his clothes and cooled him down with a damp towel.

Lina stood a few feet away whimpering. "This is all my fault. I can't believe I let this happen."

"Grab something to fan him," Kenric said.

"What?"

"I need you to fan him." He looked around the room then saw a calendar on the wall. "Use that."

Lina grabbed the calendar off the wall and used it to fan the baby.

"That's it," Kenric said in an encouraging voice as he continued to gently wipe down the baby. "Keep it up."

"Tell Carissa, I'm sorry," Lina said in a choked voice. "I'm sorry about everything."

"You'll get a chance to tell her yourself."

"She'll never want to see me again after this."

Kenric didn't get a chance to reply because the EMTs rushed in and took over. They seemed impressed by Kenric's quick thinking. "This baby is very lucky," one said. "A couple minutes more and we would have been looking at brain damage or death, but he's recovering well. We'll still take him to the hospital to monitor him."

Lina went with them in the ambulance. Glenn planned to follow in his car. But instead Kenric found him staring at the ambulance as it drove away. He made no move to follow as he wiped sweat from his forehead.

"What are you doing?" Kenric demanded.

He didn't look at him, his gaze focused on something in the distance. "Why did you save my son?" he asked in a low voice.

Kenric stiffened. "What?'

Glenn finally turned to him and Kenric saw a different man. Not the arrogant ambitious man from the past or the condescending one from a few weeks ago. He was a man who'd been humbled. "You didn't have to. Wouldn't that have been justice? An eye for an eye and all that?"

Kenric shoved his hands in his pockets and took a deep sigh. Glenn was right. He could have enacted a great revenge. But holding the limp infant in his arms made him realize something he wasn't ready to share yet. Something he knew he needed to tell his brother so that he could accept Carissa as part of their family. "You're right," he said. "But we're going to be family soon."

"I didn't kill your sister," Glenn said, not deceived by Kenric's nonchalant tone. "I swear it. I did a lot of things in my past that I'm ashamed of, but murder wasn't one of them. Understand?"

Kenric nodded.

"So tell me why. Why did you save my son?"

Kenric took his hands out of his pockets, knowing there was no point in hiding how he felt. "Because I love your sister more than I hate you," he said, then turned and walked away.

CHAPTER TWENTY-FOUR

Joshua was not a happy man when he opened the door and found Carissa York standing there. She was the second unexpected visitor he'd had that evening and he hadn't gotten rid of the first. He already had a headache and the sight of her didn't improve it.

"I'm not in the mood," he said starting to close the door.

"He's dead."

He paused, gripping the door. Damn, she got his interest and she knew it. He couldn't make her leave now. Not after a statement like that. He opened the door wider and turned away. He didn't need to ask her who, he knew she'd fill in the blanks for him. He sat down and waited.

He could tell that she was nervous as she walked to the seat facing him, but she tried to appear nonchalant. He admired her for the effort, even though she failed miserably. She looked out of her depths, her gaze quickly surveying the surroundings and seeing the opulence most of his guest didn't notice because it was expected, like seeing a gorgeous woman at a car show. His brief admiration annoyed him. He didn't want to trust her and still hated the control she seemed to have over his brother. He looked at her once again wondering what magic she'd spun to capture his brother so completely.

His brother. The thought of him made him grit his teeth. To think that Kenric still wanted to marry her. That he had the arrogance to say that he loved her. Loved! This woman who could offer him nothing. Through half closed lids he watched her sit down, resting her handbag on her lap with the primness of a nun caught in a strip club. He yawned, hoping that would give her a hint to start talking or he was going to sleep.

She took a deep breath then said, "The monster who killed your sister was called Cracker. He had a few other names, but that doesn't matter. He was a pathetic excuse for a human being who sold bad product. Unfortunately, your sister was one of his last clients."

"According to your sources?" he said with a note of sarcasm. It was a good shield against the quiet rage in her voice. A simmering rage that echoed how he felt. He didn't want her to understand, he didn't want her to sympathize with him. He wanted—needed—to see her as the enemy.

"Yes. They're reliable."

He sighed then rubbed his forehead. "If my head didn't hurt, I'd laugh."

"I can give you names of people to talk to if you're interested, but I wouldn't recommend it."

"Why not? Afraid your story might unravel?"

Her gaze didn't waver and it was at that moment he realized he'd been tricked. She wasn't as afraid as she pretended to be. "You might become a target," she said in a cool voice. But not too cool. It wasn't cold, but rather like the feel of a cool breeze on a summer day. Inviting and chilling at the same time. He had to watch himself.

"Why are you here?"

"I just thought you should know."

"That he's dead?"

She nodded. "He tried to expand into the wrong territory and got his head blown off."

"I didn't ask."

"But I knew you were curious."

Damn she was smart. Worse still, he was starting to see her allure. He could see it in that steady chocolate gaze, the beautifully shaped mouth. She wasn't even his type—he'd only tried to play her to annoy his brother, but now he was truly interested to know what she was really about. He could see why his brother had fallen for her. That was never a good thing.

"At least you know that Glenn didn't trick your brother."

He nodded, able to put his emotional shield back in place. This was why she was here. She had her own agenda. "I see. You wanted to clear your brother's name."

"No, I wanted to clear mine." She set her handbag on the ground and crossed her legs in the best power move a woman could make with a man like him. He'd noticed her legs—he always did a quick inventory of a woman, out of habit—but she brought them more into focus. She'd worn a pair of chocolate colored stockings.

He lifted his gaze to her face. Her expression hadn't changed, but the air between them certainly had and he knew why. He had to tread very carefully. He couldn't underestimate her or what the evening would turn into.

Carissa steadied her breath. She couldn't believe she'd been able to hold Joshua's attention this long. She had been careful with her words and her movements because she knew he could throw her out at any moment. Although his tone was combative and surly, she could tell that he was listening and that's all she needed. She found that she could face his distrust and disgust and not wither under it.

"I know you don't think I'm worthy of your brother and you once questioned if I really loved him," she said. "And you were right. At that moment, I didn't love him as much as I needed to. Many people talk about if you love something let it go, but there's also a flip side to that statement. Sometimes letting go is the easy way out and it takes courage to hang on. Before this moment I was willing to let him go, because I was scared to try to keep him."

"You're wasting your time telling me these things because it doesn't change anything."

"I thought you should know why I won't take your money."

Joshua suddenly seemed wide awake. He sat up and swore. "Look, you don't need to mention that."

"Didn't you say you wanted me to come up with a figure next time?"

He glanced over his shoulder then covered his eyes. "You misunderstood." He stood. "You made your point."

"You don't believe me," she said, stunned by his sudden change. "You can sit and listen to me talk about Glenn, but the moment I mention how I feel about your brother you want me to leave?"

"It's not—"

"We're meant for each other, he saw it first and was willing to fight for me and now I am too. I got lost in the details and didn't see the big picture but he always did. And I hope he will take me back and—" Her voice died away when she saw a familiar figure come from around the corner. She wanted to run into his arms, but she felt frozen in place because there was so much she wanted to say.

"How much did he offer you?" he asked.

"It was a misunderstanding," Joshua said.

Kenric casually rested his hand on his brother's shoulder and forced him back in his seat, his gaze never leaving Carissa's. "Well?"

"I don't remember," she said, her mouth dry. He was so close yet felt so far, his face unreadable. She couldn't tell how much he'd heard or what effect what she'd said had had on him. Did he think she was a liar like his brother did? But seeing him made everything else fall to the background. Nothing else mattered. She didn't care if he didn't believe her, she would try her best to convince him. "I knew that no amount of money would ever be enough." When he didn't reply and the

silence stretched between them, panic gripped her. Maybe he didn't want her anymore. Maybe she'd give him enough time to reconsider his feelings. Suddenly, all triumph left her. Standing up to James, confronting Joshua and finding out the truth about her brother wouldn't mean anything if she lost him in the end. She took a halting step forward then stopped herself, wishing she could see pass the shades of the henchman that was clear in his gaze. She took a deep breath and said, "Did you hear what I said about my brother? He-
-"

"I don't care about your brother right now," Kenric interrupted in a low tone that sent shivers through her. "I only want to know one thing."

She desperately searched her mind for possibilities eager to remove the hard mask on his face and see the man who'd once said he'd loved her. "Do you want to know if I have more information?"

He took a step forward and shook his head, but his hard gaze slowly heated holding her still. "No."

"Was I tempted?"

He took another step forward and again shook his head. "No."

"Do I have any more family secrets that—?"

He stopped a foot away from her and pressed a finger against her mouth. "No. Am I looking at my first wife?"

First wife. The relief that washed over her nearly made her knees buckle. He still wanted her. He still loved her and for the first time she realized how much she'd been afraid to accept his love and love him back. As she gazed at him, she saw that he'd never worn a mask, that it had only been her perception. His feelings had always been clear in his gaze.

She'd been the one to keep him at a distance. She had changed more than he had. He was the same man she'd hated that first day--the one whose cool demeanor she'd confused for cruelty because that was what she was used to. But he'd always been generous and loving even when no one noticed. She remembered one evening when she couldn't sleep, seeing him at her dining room table, gluing together the ugly little vase that Morris had broken. The following day he'd set the vase on the table with a bouquet of lavender roses, hot pink lilies, red spray roses surrounded by lush greens that all probably cost more than the vase was worth. He said he'd gotten the vase fixed, but she'd never told him she knew the truth.

That was the man she saw now. The man she'd fallen in love with in spite of herself. And loving him had made her a new woman, giving her strength and a bottomless joy. *First* wife. His words made life feel fresh and new and the past completely melted away.

"Carissa?" Kenric asked.

She saw a look of uneasiness enter his gaze and saw her own past fear mirrored in his gaze.

She never wanted him to doubt her love for him. She never wanted him to fear losing her again. She wrapped her arms around his neck, drawing him close, her heart hammering in her chest. "Mr. Riverton?"

"Yes?" he said with a note of caution.

"York Incorporated is ready to negotiate a possible merger."

Kenric's mouth softened into a smile. "That's good to

hear, Ms. York. Riverton International is prepared to make a very good offer."

Carissa placed a feather light kiss on his lips then whispered, "I'm listening."

Six months *later*

Carissa watched the red garter belt fly in the air. Making it part of the garter toss on her wedding day had been her final assignment for the Black Stockings Society. It soared into the eager crowd of bachelors, landing on Joshua's head. He was trying to chat up one of the bridesmaid. He tore the item off his head to the sound of laughter and sent his brother a sharp look, before tossing it away to another lucky bachelor who grabbed it and waved it in the air as a trophy.

Third time definitely was the charm. She'd had a magical wedding day. Carissa danced with her new husband amazed by all that had happened. He'd relocated to be with her, starting his own consulting firm. Lina changed her ways and let Carissa see her nephew as often as she wanted and *never* called when she didn't have to. Glenn kept his secret past from Lina and Kenric and Carissa agreed to do the same, as long as he volunteered once a week at a detox clinic and gave generously to a designated charity every year.

Carissa finished her dance with Kenric then mingled with the crowd. She looked over and saw Ashley pushing her mother's wheelchair back over to one of the tables. She was glad she'd been able to come. She walked over to her and saw tears in her eyes. "I'm so glad you could make it," Carissa said taking the older woman's hand. She remembered how vibrant she had been when Ashley was growing up and remembered how much she enjoyed babysitting at their house.

"Beautiful," was all she could manage.

"Thank you," Carissa said grabbing a napkin and wiping the woman's tears.

"Happy?"

Carissa looked over at Kenric as he laughed with Malcolm, who had been their ring bearer and looked smart dressed in a suit; her heart filled with joy. "Yes, I'm very happy," she said turning back to her.

But this time Mrs. Torville didn't reply. Instead, she held her gaze as if trying to silently communicate something to her, then she lowered her gaze.

Carissa looked down, wondering what she wanted. "Did you drop something?"

The older woman shook her head then lowered her gaze again.

Carissa again looked down and saw the woman's lovely cream dress and expensive black lace stockings. Carissa glanced up at her, with a silent question. The older woman blinked, then slowly managed a smile.

ABOUT THE AUTHOR

Dara Girard, an award-winning, national bestselling author of more than forty novels, from romance to suspense, loves telling stories.

Born in the US to immigrant parents, Dara enjoys pulling from her Jamaican, British, Nigerian heritage and exposure to various cultures to bring what reviewers and fans call "vivid emotional stories" to life. She is best known for her popular Henson Series, the mysterious Clifton Sisters, and the fun Black Stockings Society.

You can write her at:
contactdara@daragirard.com
or
P.O. Box 10345
Silver Spring, MD 20914
If you'd like to receive a reply, please send a self-addressed stamped envelope.

Visit her website to sign up for her newsletter and get sneak peeks, monthly updates on new releases, and special offers.

For more information visit
www.daragirard.com